Euthanasia

Other books in the Issues on Trial Series

Euthanasia

Mitchell Young, Book Editor

GREENHAVEN PRESS

An imprint of Thomson Gale, a part of The Thomson Corporation

Detroit • New York • San Francisco • New Haven, Conn. • Waterville, Maine • London

Christine Nasso, *Publisher*
Elizabeth Des Chenes, *Managing Editor*

© 2007 Thomson Gale, a part of The Thomson Corporation.

Thomson and Star logo are trademarks and Gale and Greenhaven Press are registered trademarks used herein under license.

For more information, contact:
Greenhaven Press
27500 Drake Rd.
Farmington Hills, MI 48331-3535
Or you can visit our Internet site at http://www.gale.com

Cover photograph reproduced by permission of Jean Louis atlan/Sygma/Corbis.

ISBN-13: 978-0-7377-2789-0
ISBN-10: 0-7377-2789-6

Library of Congress Control Number: 2007929083

Printed in the United States of America
10 9 8 7 6 5 4 3 2 1

Contents

Chapter 1: Testing the Limits of Assisted-Suicide Laws

Chapter 2: Upholding the State's Right to Ban Assisted Suicide

Chapter 3: The Schiavo Case Highlights Divisions over the Right to Die

Chapter 4: Upholding Physician-Assisted Suicide in Oregon

Foreword

The U.S. courts have long served as a battleground for the most highly charged and contentious issues of the time. Divisive matters are often brought into the legal system by activists who feel strongly for their cause and demand an official resolution. Indeed, subjects that give rise to intense emotions or involve closely held religious or moral beliefs lay at the heart of the most polemical court rulings in history. One such case was *Brown v. Board of Education* (1954), which ended racial segregation in schools. Prior to *Brown*, the courts had held that blacks could be forced to use separate facilities as long as these facilities were equal to that of whites.

For years many groups had opposed segregation based on religious, moral, and legal grounds. Educators produced heartfelt testimony that segregated schooling greatly disadvantaged black children. They noted that in comparison to whites, blacks received a substandard education in deplorable conditions. Religious leaders such as Martin Luther King Jr. preached that the harsh treatment of blacks was immoral and unjust. Many involved in civil rights law, such as Thurgood Marshall, called for equal protection of all people under the law, as their study of the Constitution had indicated that segregation was illegal and un-American. Whatever their motivation for ending the practice, and despite the threats they received from segregationists, these ardent activists remained unwavering in their cause.

Those fighting against the integration of schools were mainly white southerners who did not believe that whites and blacks should intermingle. Blacks were subordinate to whites, they maintained, and society had to resist any attempt to break down strict color lines. Some white southerners charged that segregated schooling was *not* hindering blacks' education. For example, Virginia attorney general J. Lindsay Almond asserted, "With the help and the sympathy and the love and re-spect of the white people of the South, the colored man has risen under that educational process to a place of eminence and respect throughout the nation. It has served him well." So when the Supreme Court ruled against the segregationists in *Brown*, the South responded with vociferous cries of protest. Even government leaders criticized the decision. The governor of Arkansas, Orval Faubus, stated that he would not "be a party to any attempt to force acceptance of change to which the people are so overwhelmingly opposed." Indeed, resistance to integration was so great that when black students arrived at the formerly all-white Central High School in Arkansas, fed-eral troops had to be dispatched to quell a threatening mob of protesters.

Nevertheless, the *Brown* decision was enforced and the South integrated its schools. In this instance, the Court, while not settling the issue to everyone's satisfaction, functioned as an instrument of progress by forcing a major social change. Historian David Halberstam observes that the *Brown* ruling "deprived segregationist practices of their moral legitimacy. . . . It was therefore perhaps the single most important moment of the decade, the moment that separated the old order from the new and helped create the tumultuous era just arriving." Considered one of the most important victories for civil rights, *Brown* paved the way for challenges to racial segregation in many areas, including on public buses and in restaurants.

In examining *Brown*, it becomes apparent that the courts play an influential role—and face an arduous challenge—in shaping the debate over emotionally charged social issues. Judges must balance competing interests, keeping in mind the high stakes and intense emotions on both sides. As exempli-fied by *Brown*, judicial decisions often upset the status quo and initiate significant changes in society. Greenhaven Press's Issues on Trial series captures the controversy surrounding in-fluential court rulings and explores the social ramifications of such decisions from varying perspectives. Each anthology highlights one social issue—such as the death penalty, students' rights, or wartime civil liberties. Each volume then focuses on key historical and contemporary court cases that helped mold the issue as we know it today. The books include a compendium of primary sources—court rulings, dissents, and immediate reactions to the rulings—as well as secondary sources from experts in the field, people involved in the cases, legal analysts, and other commentators opining on the implications and legacy of the chosen cases. An annotated table of contents, an in-depth introduction, and prefaces that overview each case all provide context as readers delve into the topic at hand. To help students fully probe the subject, each volume contains book and periodical bibliographies, a comprehensive index, and a list of organizations to contact. With these features, the Issues on Trial series offers a well-rounded perspective on the courts' role in framing society's thorniest, most impassioned debates.

Introduction

Euthanasia (from the Greek for "good death") is an issue that involves medical, legal, financial, religious, and moral concerns; however, the most difficult problem is determining who decides when a life is not worth living. Already much heard in the debate over abortion, the catch phrase "who decides?" has now become part of the euthanasia controversy as well.

Proponents of physician-assisted suicide believe the decision whether to live or die should be left to the individual. They hold that all persons have the right to decide when and how to end their struggle with terminal illness. For supporters, the gradual expansion of personal liberty—the right of the individual to control his or her own body—justifies legalizing euthanasia.

Opponents frame the issue in terms of euthanasia's history and argue that legal assisted suicide will result in "mercy killings" that are not truly voluntary. They believe that the most vulnerable in society will be victimized by legal euthanasia. They point to Adolf Hitler's Germany, in which those deemed "unfit" because of illness were euthanized long before the systematic murder of Jews and other disapproved-of groups began. As author Kirk Cheyfitz has written, the "suicide, euthanasia, infanticide, eugenics, genocide and, most recently, the practice termed physician-assisted suicide" all come down "to two troublesome questions: Which lives are not worth living? And who will decide?"[1]

Since the 1990s these questions have been hotly debated in U.S. courts. Right-to-die activists, inspired by Supreme Court decisions that emphasized the right to "bodily autonomy," claim that the terminally ill have the ultimate say over their own manner of death. These activists are determined to convince the public that assisted suicide is a matter of individual choice. In the early nineties, polls showed support for Dr. Jack Kevorkian, who was beginning to help "patients" commit suicide. Moreover, despite the passage of a state law prohibiting assisted suicide, three Michigan juries refused to convict him. In Oregon voters approved Measure 16, the Death with Dignity Act, in 1994. Governor John Kitzhaber spoke for many Oregonians when he defended the act, saying "I believe an individual should have control, should be able to make choices about the end of their life."[2]

Nevertheless, by the end of the 1990s, opponents of physician-assisted suicide were able to muster some support for the position that the public had the right to outlaw assisted suicide. They did not directly confront the claim that individuals should be able to decide the course of their own end-of-life treatment. Instead, they argued that in many instances, the terminally ill individual would not truly have a free choice. Financial pressures from hospitals and even family members would put pressure on the ill person to end their lives quickly. As Wesley J. Smith, attorney for the International Task Force on Euthanasia and Assisted Suicide, put it:

> When a doctor killing his patient becomes an ordinary affair, assisted suicide could be seen as an easy way to cut medical costs, thereby increasing profits for HMOs [health maintenance organizations] while reducing financial burdens on taxpayers who pay for government health care programs and families who care for ill and disabled members.[3]

Opponents held that the state has not only the right but the obligation to prohibit assisted suicide in order to protect the poor and vulnerable in society. The pressure to request euthanasia would be greatest on these groups because of their lack of money; in the long run they would be more likely to be euthanized. Smith notes that some groups who work with the poor had already begun working against the legalization of physician-assisted suicide precisely because they anticipated the poor would be victimized.

In the Supreme Court's 1997 case *Washington v. Glucksberg* the two sides clashed over who had the legitimate right to make end-of-life decisions. As usual, proponents of physician-assisted suicide asserted an individual right to bodily autonomy. The American Civil Liberties Union (ACLU) wrote in its amicus curiae ("friend of the court") brief:

> The right of a competent, terminally ill person to avoid excruciating pain and embrace a timely and dignified death bears the sanction of history and is implicit in the concept of ordered liberty. The exercise of this right is as central to personal autonomy and bodily integrity as rights safeguarded by this Court's decision.[4]

Despite the ACLU's position, the Supreme Court ruled that the people of the various states had a right to decide, through their state legislatures or directly through ballot initiatives (referendums) whether to outlaw or permit physician-assisted suicide. The decision gave citizens, acting through the democratic process, the responsibility of balancing the right of the individual to obtain relief from suffering with the obligation of the state to protect the vulnerable. As Justice Sandra Day O'Connor wrote in her concurring opinion,

> There is no reason to think the democratic process will not strike the proper balance between the interests of terminally ill, mentally competent individuals who would seek to end their suffering and the State's interests in protecting those who might seek to end life mistakenly or under pressure.[5]

The Supreme Court's ruling in *Washington v. Glucksberg* cleared the way for Michigan voters to reject physician-assisted suicide, which they did in a November 1998 election. Perhaps they were made more aware of the dangers inherent in assisted suicide by Dr. Jack Kevorkian's activities; he had assisted in the suicide of one hundred people, some of whom were not terminally ill.

Though the Supreme Court had ruled that the state could legalize assisted suicide, this was not the final decision on this public policy issue. In contrast with Michigan, voters in Oregon were determined to keep their Death with Dignity law. They rejected an attempt to overturn the law via ballot initiative. When attorney general John Ashcroft attempted to limit the ability of terminally ill patients to receive drugs for assisted suicide by declaring the drugs' prescription for such a violation of federal drug laws, the state attorney defended the law. Again the Supreme Court ruled in favor of letting the people of the various states decide the matter; Ashcroft's directive was declared invalid in *Gonzales v. Oregon* (2006).

Just as the federal and state governments have clashed over the legal right to make policy on euthanasia, families argue over who has the right to decide for incapacitated patients. According to bioethicist Bruce Jennings, in the first major case of this kind, the New Jersey Supreme Court said, "Make the decisions at the bedside, with the patient if possible, or with the family ... with the physician; make the decision as close to the bedside as you possibly can."[6] But at times the family itself is in disagreement. The heart of the 2005 Theresa (Terri) Schiavo case was the disagreement between the husband and Terri's parents over the decision to maintain artificial feeding and hydration. The Schindlers (Terri's parents) believed that they should be allowed to decide Terri's fate since her husband, Michael Schiavo, had financial and emotional incentives to let Terri die. Schiavo thought he should decide because he felt that he knew best what his wife's wishes would have been. The courts ultimately gave Michael Schiavo the right to decide his wife's fate; he chose to have artificial feeding and hydration stopped—technically not an act of euthanasia but an act of "letting die."

The Schiavo controversy caused a clash between branches of government. The Florida Supreme Court and the United States Supreme Court both rejected the attempts of the executive and legislative branches to interfere with the lower courts' rulings. In the end, the courts ruled that it was they who decided "who gets to decide"; neither the legislative nor the executive branches could overturn judicial decisions in this regard.

U.S. Supreme Court rulings have held that the people of the various states possess the ultimate right to decide whether or not euthanasia is legal. In one state—Oregon—the people have given that right to the individual, while in many other states voters have explicitly rejected a right to assisted suicide. While euthanasia remains a crime throughout most of the nation, activists from Oregon and elsewhere still work to promote their view that the individual has the right to decide whether to live or die. No doubt legal battles over this issue will continue long into the future.

Notes

1. Kirk Cheyfitz, "Who Decides? The Connecting Thread of Euthanasia, Eugenics, and Doctor-Assisted Suicide," *Omega, Journal of Death and Dying*, vol. 40, no. 1, 1999.
2. Quoted in "Arguments in Opposition" [to Measure 51], Oregon Ballot, *Sunday Oregonian*, August 2, 1997, November 4, 1997.
3. Wesley J. Smith, "Suicide Pays," *First Things: A Monthly Journal of Religion and Public Life*, June 1999.
4. American Civil Liberties Union, Amicus Brief in *Vacco v. Quill*, December 10, 1996.
5. Sandra Day O'Connor, concurring opinion, *Washington v. Glucksberg*, 1997.
6. Bruce Jennings, "The Long Dying of Terri Schiavo—Private Tragedy, Public Danger," Garrison Colloquium, The Hastings Center (www.thehastingscenter.org/news/features/schiavojennings.asp).

CHAPTER 1

Testing the Limits of Assisted-Suicide Laws

Case Overview

People of Michigan v. Jack Kevorkian (1994)

Dr. Jack Kevorkian is almost single-handedly responsible for bringing the issue of physician-assisted suicide to the attention of the American public. Beginning in the late 1980s, Kevorkian went on a campaign to legalize physician-assisted suicide. He practiced what he preached by helping the terminally ill to commit suicide with his "mercy machine," a do-it-yourself device for administering lethal injections.

In February 1993, after several deaths involving Kevorkian, the governor of Michigan signed a law banning assisted suicide that had been passed by the state legislature. Prosecutors soon brought a series of charges against Kevorkian for violating the ban; however, he was acquitted by a jury in one trial, while several lower courts in Michigan ruled that the state ban on assisted suicide was an unconstitutional interference with an individual's "right to die."

The Michigan attorney general appealed the lower courts' decisions to the Michigan Supreme Court. That court ruled, in a decision written by Justice Michael F. Cavanaugh, that the United States Constitution did not contain a right to die by assisted suicide. Nor did the history of the American people or current attitudes justify finding such a right. Cavanaugh held that while judges could find rights not explicitly in the Constitution, they must be rooted in American tradition, and there was no tradition of legal assisted suicide in the United States. In fact, historically and currently most states have specifically banned the practice. Therefore, Cavanaugh argued, the Michigan lower courts were wrong in finding that the Michigan ban on assisted suicide violated a constitutional right to die.

Cavanaugh's opinion treated assisted sucide as a matter of public policy that was best left to the voters and their elected representatives. Indeed, in 1994, while the case was being decided, voters in the state of Oregon passed the Death with Dignity Act. Later, the citizens of California and Washington rejected right-to-die laws. It was the decision in *People of Michigan v. Jack Kevorkian* that left the door open for continuing public debate on the matter. Subsequent U.S. Supreme Court decisions, especially *Washington v. Glucksberg* (1997), confirmed the basic finding of the Michigan court that states could ban assisted suicide. Oregon has stuck with its legalization of physician-assisted suicide, but other states continue to reject such a policy.

In 1999, five years after the state supreme court ruling, Kevorkian was convicted of murder under a second law passed in Michigan that explicitly forbade assisted suicide (the earlier ban had expired). The judge in that trial was scathing, accusing Kevorkian of daring the Michigan court system to stop him. "Well, consider yourself stopped," stated the judge at Kevorkian's last trial. He was sentenced to ten to twenty-five years in prison. (He was paroled in December 2006.)

Despite his conviction, Kevorkian still has his supporters, including families of those he helped commit suicide. In an era when medical technology can prolong·life, even of the gravely ill, Kevorkian's dramatic behavior intensified the debate over euthanasia in the United States.

"The fact of the matter is that doctors assist their patients to commit suicide every day of the year."

Dr. Jack Kevorkian Advocates the Legalization of Assisted Suicide

Melvin I. Urofsky

Melvin I. Urofsky is a professor of public policy at Virginia Commonwealth University. He has written or edited several works on euthanasia, including Letting Go: Death, Dying and the Law *and* The Right to Die, *a two-volume anthology of scholarly articles.*

In the following excerpt from his book Lethal Judgments: Assisted Suicide and American Law, *Urofsky gives an overview of Dr. Jack Kevorkian's first activities in Michigan, including his first brushes with the law. In 1990, after assisting a fifty-four-year-old woman to take her life, the pathologist came to the attention of the Oakland County, Michigan, prosecutor's office. He was charged with murder but released when a jury failed to convict him. This was the beginning of a series of run-ins with the law as Kevorkian continued to promote the cause of physician-assisted suicide not only through speeches but by performing acts of "mercy killing." The media soon began referring to Kevorkian by the nickname he received as a young doctor who studied dying patients—"Dr. Death."*

While Urofsky does not explicitly endorse physician-assisted suicide, the tone of this excerpt is generally sympathetic toward

Kevorkian. The excerpt contains several passages from Kevorkian's supporters, who saw him as the only hope for a dignified death under terrible circumstances.

The debate over physician-assisted suicide often begins—and ends—with the activities of Jack Kevorkian, the so-called Dr. Death who has reportedly assisted more than 130 people to end their lives. But the issues involved transcend the activities of the retired pathologist. He has pushed the envelope and offended many people, but he has also become a hero to those who believe that society ignores the needs and the wishes of those for whom life no longer has any value. Most important, Kevorkian has forced a public debate over the options people should have at the end of life.

Kevorkian Gains Notoriety

On June 4, 1990, in a van parked in a public park outside Detroit, Dr. Jack Kevorkian hooked up what he called his "Mercy Machine" to 54-year-old Janet Adkins, a Portland, Oregon, school-teacher suffering from the early stages of Alzheimer's disease. Ms. Adkins had read about Kevorkian, a longtime advocate of physician-assisted suicide, and she had contacted him in the fall of 1989. After some correspondence and phone calls, Kevorkian agreed to help her end her life, and Janet Adkins and her husband Ron flew east to meet with him. To make sure that she understood exactly what she was doing, Kevorkian set up a videocamera in a hotel room, and recorded a forty-minute conversation with the woman:

> *Kevorkian*: How was your life before, and how is it different now?
>
> *Adkins*: My life was wonderful before, because I could play the piano. I could read. And I can't do any of those things [anymore]. . . .
>
> *Kevorkian*: Janet, you know what you're asking me to do?

Adkins: Yes.

Kevorkian: You realize that . . . You want help from me. . . . You realize that I can make arrangements for everything, and you would have to do it. That you would have to push the button.

Adkins: I understand.

Kevorkian: Janet, are you aware of your decision, and the implications of your decision?

Adkins: Yes.

Kevorkian: What does it mean?

Adkins: That I can get out with dignity.

The next morning, Kevorkian showed Janet Adkins his device, three vials suspended over a metal box containing a small electric motor. Once the doctor had inserted an intravenous tube into her arm, she could press a button that would start the flow of saline solution; then it would open the valve to the second vial, releasing thiopental, which would induce unconsciousness; finally, the contents of the third vial, potassium chloride, would cause her heart to stop.

Kevorkian again asked Janet Adkins if she understood what would happen, if she wanted to go ahead, if she knew what to do. She assured him she did. Kevorkian attached an electrocardiograph and left the van; when he came back a little while later, Ms. Adkins was dead. The retired pathologist then called the police and reported the death.

"Dr. Death" Faces Legal Sanctions

The story of "Dr. Death," as the media soon labeled him, exploded all over the nation's newspapers and television stations. Doctors, ethicists, and laypeople alike all had something to say, and so did the law. Oakland County [Michigan] assistant prosecutor Michael Modelsky sought a first-degree murder charge, but after a two-day preliminary hearing, Judge Gerald McNally ruled that the state had failed to prove that Kevorkian had planned and carried out the death of the woman. Ms. Adkins, McNally noted, had caused her own death, and since Michigan had no prohibition against assisting in a suicide, Kevorkian had broken no law. But obviously appalled at the event, McNally called upon the state legislature to address the issue.

Then in January 1991, Modelsky filed a civil suit to stop Kevorkian from using his device in the future. The four-day trial heard testimony from doctors, who denounced Kevorkian for violating medical ethics, as well as from people who praised the "Mercy Machine" and wanted the legal opportunity to use it. Dr. Arthur Caplan, of the University of Minnesota Center for Biomedical Ethics, said Kevorkian's actions fell "well outside acceptable practice for physicians" and that they would undermine the public's view of "doctors as people they can trust, who will not abuse their power and take life unnecessarily." Actually, opinion within medical circles seemed to be split on the case. Although many doctors criticized Kevorkian's handling of the Adkins situation, they did not necessarily disapprove of his intent. A survey by the New York–based *Medical Tribune* found about 45 percent approved of Kevorkian's actions.

Patients and Families Support Kevorkian

To defend Dr. Kevorkian's actions as humane and compassionate, defense attorney Geoffrey Fieger called Sherry Miller to the stand. Mrs. Miller, the 42-year-old mother of two teenagers, had been battling the crippling effects of multiple sclerosis for more than a dozen years, and she could not even lift her hand to take the oath. She described the ravages of the disease: "I went from a cane to a walker to a wheelchair. I can't walk. I can't write. . . . I can't function as a human being.

What can anybody do? Nothing. I want the right to die." Medical science had been unable to help her, and Kevorkian's machine now seemed her only hope. "I should have done something sooner when I was more—when I was capable of doing something on my own." When asked if she could not do something on her own now, Ms. Miller said no. "I can't take a bunch of pills because I can't get to them," and she did not have the strength or the coordination to use a gun.

The attorney then asked what she thought of the statements by some of the medical ethicists who had testified that people who are in pain or have terminal illnesses can be made more comfortable through medical treatment, so there is no need to end their lives. "You sit in this chair for a year," she said, "not being able to do anything, and being made comfortable, and then tell me. You know, the quality of life after you sit in here—in my chair."

The defense called other witnesses who related how Kevorkian's machine offered them their only hope out of a nightmarish situation. Virginia Bernero told of her son Victor's four-year battle with AIDS, and his great pain and suffering. They saw a story about Kevorkian on television, and Victor said he wanted to use the machine. Victor had died in November 1990, and his family said he suffered needlessly; to them, as her other son, Virgil, said, Kevorkian is "a hero and a trailblazer in a field of processionary caterpillars."

Michigan Law Unclear on Physician-Assisted Suicide

Although a Michigan lawmaker had promised to introduce legislation to govern such cases, Judge Alice Gilbert [who was trying the civil case] had no statute in place to guide her decision. But law libraries are far from devoid of information and cases dealing with aiding, abetting, or counseling suicide. Under common law, if one counseled another to commit suicide, that person could be held guilty of aiding and abetting murder. If present at the time of the actual death, the adviser could be charged as a principal in the second degree; if not present, then he or she in all likelihood would go free, even though technically an accessory before the fact. The reason the adviser would escape punishment lies in the common law rule that an accessory cannot be tried for a crime unless the perpetrator has been convicted, and obviously, one cannot try a successful suicide.

The great English jurist [William] Blackstone believed, however, that "if one persuades another to kill himself, and he does so, the advisor is guilty of murder," and a few states have adopted that view. Also, in so-called suicide pacts, if two persons agree to kill themselves together and only one dies, the survivor is considered guilty of the murder of the one who dies.

In a federal system such as ours, it is possible for events that are legal—or at least noncriminal—in one state to be outlawed in another. Jack Kevorkian escaped criminal charges because Michigan had no statute addressing assisted suicide, but had he set up his machine in Missouri or Oregon he might well have been indicted and convicted as an accessory to murder.

Judge Gilbert eventually issued an injunction against Kevorkian's using the machine to help other people commit suicide. "His goal is self-service rather than patient service," she charged, and his fellow physicians "look upon him as a menace that threatens the existence of the medical profession." Although Kevorkian pronounced himself saddened by the ruling, he initially promised to abide by it, although "I can still speak out and promulgate ideas." One day later, however, he was counseling a cancer-stricken dentist about suicide and announcing that he would test the limits of the injunction. Then, in October 1991, as one news magazine put it, "Dr. Death Strikes Again."

Victimized by Disease and Society

One can hardly describe the two women involved as "murder victims." If anything, they saw themselves victimized by cruel diseases and a society that denied them the one release they sought. Marjorie Wantz, 58, suffered from a painful pelvic disorder; she had endured ten operations, none of which had helped, and had been housebound for more than three years. Neighbors said that her cries of pain could often be heard at night. She had met Kevorkian on a Detroit talk show and then had read the surprising runaway best-seller *Final Exit*, a how-to-do-it suicide manual by Hemlock Society founder Derek Humphry. She had tried to follow the instructions in the book and had failed; so she turned to Kevorkian and his machine. The other woman, Sherry Miller, 43, had testified at Kevorkian's trial; she did not have the strength left even to push the button, so Kevorkian arranged for her to breathe carbon monoxide through a mask, while her best friend sat at her side. Kevorkian was present at the cabin in Bald Mountain Park, about forty miles north of Detroit, and after both women had died, he called the police. When the county sheriff arrived, the bodies were still hooked up to the machines. Kevorkian's lawyer, Geoffrey Fieger, noted that his client "provided the expertise. He provided the equipment." Asked whether he expected Kevorkian to be prosecuted, Fieger said "No . . . it's a humane, ethical, medical act."

Kevorkian remained free of criminal charges; the state assembly, despite the extensive publicity surrounding the death of Janet Adkins, had failed to enact any legislation on assisted suicide. Prosecutors tried to indict him on murder charges for assisting Marjorie Wantz and Sherry Miller to commit suicide, but failed. When they did manage to bring him to trial on a later indictment, the jury refused to convict. Eventually Michigan prosecutors gave up, recognizing that even if they could secure a grand jury indictment, petit juries would not convict him. Whatever moral judgment one wishes to make about his behavior, he did not violate Michigan law as it then stood.

Kevorkian Promotes Right-to-Die Cause

Kevorkian's case is unique in that he sees himself as an advocate and seeks publicity for his cause. The fact of the matter is that doctors assist their patients to commit suicide every day of the year. Most of them do so quietly and indirectly, with perhaps only the family knowing or guessing the truth. The columnist Anna Quindlen recalled a conversation she had once had with a friend whose mother suffered from the pain of ovarian cancer. Her friend spoke of the wonderful oncologist treating her mother, and how kind and patient and considerate he was, but those were not his greatest virtues. "He told me how many of my mother's painkillers constituted a lethal dose.". . .

Doctors are sworn to protect life, but far more than most people in society, they see death. They see people so diseased and wracked with pain that death is preferable to life, and they are unique in having the power and the resources to bring that release. Although some newspapers condemned Kevorkian for "disgracing" the medical profession, doctors may, both legally and ethically, help patients to die.

The doctor who agrees to forgo treatment, or to help patients avoid further treatment, is not assisting in suicide. Courts have consistently ruled that forgoing treatment is not suicide, because the act of refusing treatment is not the cause of death; people die from their illness, not from withdrawal of treatment. Suicide is self-inflicted death; the illness that leads to death is not self-inflicted.

To some people, this appears as sophistry, the drawing of fine lines to disguise or rationalize murder. But the law is made of fine distinctions, not just in the criminal area but in civil law as well. One has to take into account the facts of the situation, the motives of the actors, the rights of both society and the individual. Nor is the law immune from morality or compassion, and that is as it ought to be.

> "A right [to commit suicide] is not expressly recognized anywhere in the United States Constitution or in the decisions of the United States Supreme Court."

The Court's Decision: Assisted Suicide Is Not a Constitutional Right

Michael F. Cavanagh

In 1992 the Michigan state legislature, motivated by Dr. Jack Kevorkian's activities, passed a law against assisted suicide. According to Kevorkian's attorney, the Supreme Court decisions in Cruzan v. Director, Missouri Department of Health *(1990) and* Planned Parenthood v. Casey *(1992) implied that the new law was unconstitutional, as was the prosecution of Kevorkian.*

In the following extract, then-Michigan chief justice Michael F. Cavanagh reverses a lower court decision that ruled in favor of a constitutional right to assisted suicide.

According to Cavanagh's ruling, nowhere in the Casey *or* Cruzan *decisions or the Constitution itself are judges authorized to establish a right to assisted suicide. While new rights can be found by judges, they must evolve rationally from the "deeply rooted history and tradition," as the Supreme Court put it, of the people. Because most states had longtime bans on assisted suicide, and historically American law punished both suicide and those who assisted suicide, there was no basis for the "rational evolution" of a right to suicide from American tradition.*

Michael F. Cavanagh, majority opinion, *People of Michigan v. Jack Kevorkian*, December 13, 1994.

The Michigan Supreme Court's decision essentially sent the issue of assisted suicide back to the people. Cavanagh suggests, in the last paragraph of the excerpt, that since assisted suicide is a matter of basic public policy, it is best resolved either by state legislatures or by direct vote of the people via state ballot initiatives.

Michael F. Cavanagh was first elected to the Michigan Supreme Court in 1982 and served as chief justice from 1991 to 1995.

The state argues that in determining those fundamental rights not expressly identified in, but nonetheless protected by, the Due Process Clause, the analysis must be guided by a search for whether the asserted right is implicit in the concept of ordered liberty or deeply rooted in our nation's history and traditions.

New Rights Must Evolve Rationally

Those who urge this court to find a fundamental liberty interest in suicide under the Due Process Clause challenge the traditional analysis, arguing that the United States Supreme Court articulated in *Casey* a new, broader inquiry to be employed in the adjudication of substantive due process claims. They submit that even if such a right cannot be inferred from *Casey*, it nonetheless exists as a rational extension of those liberty interests previously recognized under a principled application of the proper test for determining whether an asserted right is protected by the Due Process Clause.

We acknowledge that the United States Supreme Court said in *Casey* that courts are to exercise reasoned judgment in assessing claims of substantive due process, and that the analysis is "not susceptible of expression as a simple rule." However, we need not resolve the debate over whether the Court established a new test because further examination of the principles discussed in *Casey* reveals that the constitutional inquiry described in that case does not fall so far outside the "implicit in the concept of ordered liberty" and "deeply rooted in history and tradition" analysis as to lead to a different conclusion here. . . .

[W]e must determine whether the asserted right to commit suicide arises from a rational evolution of tradition, or whether recognition of such a right would be a radical departure from historical precepts. We conclude that the principles that guide analysis of substantive due process do not support the recognition of a right to commit suicide.

Nearly All States Have Punished Assisted Suicide

Although acts of suicide are documented throughout the recorded history of England and this nation, we find no indication of widespread societal approval. To the contrary, suicide was a criminal offense, with significant stigmatizing consequences. As a policy matter, and for practical reasons, suicide was not criminalized in most states. Lawmakers recognized the futility of punishment and the harshness of property forfeiture and other consequences.

Also, it was assumed that one who committed suicide was suffering from a mental frailty of one sort or another, and thus lacked the necessary *mens rea* [guilty mind] to commit a crime.

One who assisted a suicide was accorded no such concession, however. At the time the Fourteenth Amendment was ratified, at least twenty-one of the thirty-seven existing states (including eighteen of the thirty ratifying states) proscribed assisted suicide either by statute or as a common-law offense.

Presently, a substantial number of jurisdictions have specific statutes that criminalize assisted suicide, and the Model Penal Code also provides for criminal penalties. Further, nearly all states expressly disapprove of suicide and assisted suicide either in statutes dealing with durable powers of attorney in health-care situations, or in "living will" statutes. In addition, all states provide for the involuntary commitment of persons who may harm themselves as the result of mental illness, and a number of states allow the use of nondeadly force to thwart suicide attempts.

No Right to Suicide in the Constitution

It is thus incorrect to conclude, on the basis of the absence of criminal penalties for an act of suicide itself and the existence of a pragmatic capacity to commit suicide, that there is a constitutional right to commit suicide. Such a right is not expressly recognized anywhere in the United States Constitution or in the decisions of the United States Supreme Court and cannot be reasonably inferred. In fact, . . . those courts that have found a right to refuse to begin or to continue life-sustaining medical treatment have done so only after concluding that such refusal is wholly different from an act of suicide.

Indeed, the United States Supreme Court repeatedly and unequivocally has affirmed the sanctity of human life and rejected the notion that there is a right of self-destruction inherent in any common law doctrine or constitutional phrase. In *Cruzan*, the majority observed:

> As a general matter, the States—indeed, all civilized nations—demonstrate their commitment to life by treating homicide as a serious crime. Moreover, the majority of States in this country have laws imposing criminal penalties on one who assists another to commit suicide. We do not think a State is required to remain neutral in the face of an informed and voluntary decision by a physically able adult to starve to death.

On the basis of the foregoing analysis, we would hold that the right to commit suicide is neither implicit in the concept of ordered liberty nor deeply rooted in this nation's history and tradition. It would be an impermissibly radical departure from existing tradition, and from the principles that underlie that tradition, to declare that there is such a fundamental right protected by the Due Process Clause.

We are keenly aware of the intense emotions and competing moral philosophies that characterize the present debate about suicide in general, and assisted suicide in particular. The issues do not lend themselves to simple answers. However, while the complexity of the matter does not permit us to avoid the critical constitutional questions, neither does it, under the guise of constitutional interpretation, permit us to expand the judicial powers of this Court, especially where the question clearly is a policy one that is appropriately left to the citizenry for resolution, either through its elected representatives or through a ballot initiative.

> "I would hold that the plaintiffs may assert a constitutional right to physician-assisted suicide if it can be shown that they have made a competent decision and are suffering from great pain."

Dissenting Opinion: Supreme Court Decisions Imply a Constitutional Right to Assisted Suicide

Conrad L. Mallett, Jr.

In his concurring opinion (which a judge writes when he or she agrees with the court's final decision but not on how it was argued or arrived at), Michigan Supreme Court justice Conrad L. Mallett, Jr. agrees with the court's majority opinion that Kevorkian can be tried for assisting a suicide. However, Mallett sharply disagrees with the majority that the state's blanket ban on assisted suicide is legal. He makes the case that the state does have interests in safeguarding the lives of its citizens, preventing suicide in general, and maintaining the standards of the medical profession, but that as terminal illness progresses and a patient is undergoing suffering, the state's interests diminish. The state's interests must be balanced against the interest of the terminally ill patient who is suffering great pain, and has a right to die with dignity. According to Mallett, the blanket ban on physician-assisted suicide passed by the Michigan state legislature does not attempt to balance these interests and is therefore unconstitu-

Conrad L. Mallett, Jr., dissenting (in part) opinion, *People of Michigan v. Jack Kevorkian*, December 13, 1994.

tional. Justice Mallett was elected to the Michigan Supreme Court in 1990. He served until 1998, resigning his seat on the bench to become active in Detroit politics.

D r. [Jack] Kevorkian asks this Court to find that there is a constitutional right for a suffering person to commit suicide with the assistance of a physician. However, I do not believe that people can always make competent decisions regarding their fate while suffering, because too often there are circumstances in which such decisions would be later regarded as mistakes.

No Absolute Right to Assisted Suicide

Plaintiffs [Kevorkian and his codefendants] ask this Court to recognize that a terminally ill person has a fundamental right to hasten an inevitable death. To the extent that the plaintiff asks this Court to recognize that a terminally ill person has an absolute right to make a choice to hasten an inevitable death, I believe this swings the pendulum too far. Instead, I would conclude that a terminally ill person has such a right only if the person has made a competent decision and is suffering from great pain. Because plaintiffs are in a position to meet such a requirement, the Court ought not allow the prospect of reversal by the United States Supreme Court to inhibit the analysis of the very real constitutional claims presented by the plaintiffs. Beyond th[ese] criteria, I would hold that the state may assert its interest to preserve life as well as other established interests. Therefore, because the statute completely prohibits physician-assisted suicide, I believe that it is facially invalid.

This, of course, is not to say that the state does not have a readily identifiable interest in this area. The state has a legitimate interest in the preservation of the lives of its citizenry. However, the interests are not all-encompassing interests that would allow a blanket ban on physician-assisted suicide. [U.S. Supreme Court justice William Brennan wrote:] "The Constitution imposes on this Court the obligation to 'examine carefully . . . the extent to which [the legitimate government interests advanced] are served by the challenged regulation.'" The interest in the preservation of life that is advanced by the state in the present case is not served by preserving the life of a person who will inevitably die and is suffering intolerable pain.

While it is arguable that each of us possesses the right to commit suicide because suicide is no longer criminally punishable, such a right, if it exists, is not absolute when a third party is involved. Indeed, protecting the rights and interests of third parties underpins both our constitutional doctrine and criminal laws. Accordingly, I do not embrace the suggestion that because a person may have the right to commit suicide, he also has an unconditional constitutional right to physician-assisted suicide. Rather, the right to physician-assisted suicide must be balanced against the countervailing interests of the state and society.

Area of State Interest

There are four main interests in this area that may be asserted by the state: (1) the preservation of life, (2) the protection of innocent third parties, (3) the prevention of suicide, and (4) the maintenance of the ethical integrity of the medical profession. [Court rulings] have uniformly maintained that a "'state's interest in the preservation of life has been held to be insufficient to outweigh the individual right where the life which would be preserved would be one in a merely vegetative state or one enduring only a prolonged process of dying. . . .'" Similarly, there does not exist a sufficiently compelling justification for the infringement of the right of a competent, terminally ill person suffering from great pain to hasten death through physician-prescribed medications.

As a person's illness progresses to the point of facing an inevitable death while suffering great pain, the state cannot put forth a sufficient rationale to completely proscribe physician-assisted suicide. In *Brophy v. New England Sinai Hospital* (1986), the Massachusetts Supreme Judicial Court balanced the state's interest in the preservation of human life against the right of self-determination and individual autonomy. The court noted that the state's interest ordinarily involves the prolongation of human life and that that interest is "very high when 'human life [can] be saved where the affliction is curable.'" However, the court further noted that this interest diminishes as the prognosis for recovery wanes. Thus, when a person is suffering from a terminal disease, the state should avoid subjective judgments concerning the quality of that person's life.

The state may also require that such decisions be made competently. Such a requirement has been fashioned by previous courts as well. In *Application of President & Directors of Georgetown College, Inc.*, (1964), the court denied the right of patients to refuse lifesaving treatment for themselves in circumstances strongly suggesting that they lack the time or the capacity for reflection on the matter, so that the course least likely to do irreversible harm was an insistence on proceeding with treatment. . . .

Kevorkian Has Acted Within Area of State's Interest

Dr. Kevorkian's actions are within the scope of the state's protected interests. To the extent that a country sanctions the assisted suicide of the suffering, it does so at the risk of harm to its most vulnerable of citizens; e.g., the elderly and the clinically depressed.

Furthermore, extending the right to any suffering person making a rational decision almost begs the question. It has been widely acknowledged that most individuals who attempt suicide are suffering from depression, hopelessness, or lack of social interaction. Often such attempts are merely "cries for help." There are also socioeconomic pressures on individuals that make them consider suicide as a means of relief. Circumstances such as grief, prejudice, oppression, or teenage stress are often the reasons cited by people attempting suicide.

Therefore, the state has a right to legislate in this area. However, the state's interests diminish as death nears for a terminally ill person; the interests are no longer sufficient to outweigh an individual's right to self-determination. Such an outcome would be consistent with *Compassion in Dying* [*v. State of Washington*, the lower court's case name for *Washington v. Glucksberg* (1996)], in which the court recognized the right of mentally competent, terminally ill adults to knowingly and voluntarily hasten their deaths.

Absolute Ban on Assisted Suicide Is Unconstitutional

The statute at issue should be deemed facially invalid because it bans all assisted suicides. A terminally ill individual who is suffering from great pain and who has made a competent decision should have a constitutional due process right to hasten his death. Because plaintiffs are in a position to now make a choice that I believe should survive any challenge from the state, I would hold that the statute represents an undue burden on that right.

The assumption that the recognition of this right would be problematic in its administration is not an appropriate consideration when determining the existence of a fundamental right. Indeed, constitutional litigation often creates the necessity to draw abstract lines that in practice are not easily workable. Nevertheless, the recognition of fundamental rights requires choices in these areas that are not readily ascribable to any particular administrative device.

We need only look to the development of the living will as an example of guidelines in the death and dying area that work effectively and remain constitutional. [A] competent person already has the right to document the desire to refuse lifesaving medical treatment. While such documentation provides us with the right to refuse life-sustaining treatment, our laws currently do not permit us to choose to end our suffering as we near death through physician-prescribed medications. If we were allowed such an opportunity, our own reasoned judgment would prevail in each case.

There is no adequate distinction between the right of a terminally ill person to refuse unwanted medical treatment and the right to physician-assisted suicide. There is no sense in disallowing the competent choice to have a physician intervene to relieve intolerable suffering at the end of one's life. Furthermore, such a result conflicts with what many of us would desire when faced with severe pain and an inevitable death.

Citizens Are Disturbed by Kevorkian's Crusade

Many citizens of this state are disturbed by defendant Kevorkian's crusade and, at the same time, wish to see a resolution of the difficulties facing the terminally ill. Perhaps even more troubling is that, under this law, an individual is forbidden from consulting with a private, trusted physician about such matters. The recognition of a right to make such private decisions with a trusted physician would allow open and honest discussion with the patient of all options and consequences.

Substantive due process cases invariably address those rights that are considered so fundamental that they cannot be unduly burdened by the state. Here, it is fundamentally wrong not to allow a competent, terminally ill person who is suffering from great pain the opportunity to die with some dignity.

Therefore, I would hold that the plaintiffs may assert a constitutional right to physician-assisted suicide if it can be shown that they have made a competent decision and are suffering from great pain. I would further allow, consistent with

Cruzan [*v. Director, Missouri Department of Health* (1990)], that the state may require proof of such a competent decision by clear and convincing evidence if it chooses to so legislate.

| *"Dr. Jack Kevorkian should be regarded as a hero."*

Terminally Ill Patients Need Options

Frank A. Oski

Frank A. Oski wrote the following article in 1994 for The Nation, *during the controversy surrounding Dr. Kevorkian's case for physician-assisted suicide. Oski argues that Kevorkian is acting as a humanitarian in offering terminally ill patients the option to end years of suffering. He maintains that patients need new options to end suffering, and that if nothing else, Kevorkian's case should raise awareness and revive debate in America surrounding the needs of terminally ill patients.*

"What we need is a brave doctor and a case which will convince the judiciary that reform is required," said British psychiatrist Colin Brewer at the sixth biennial conference of the World Federation of Right to Die Societies in 1986. We now have that brave doctor, twenty cases of physician-assisted suicide and considerable public tumult.

Kevorkian Acts Out of Humanity

Dr. Jack Kevorkian should be regarded as a hero. He has taken on the tough issue that many physicians have avoided despite the pleas of anguished patients. We have legitimized advance directives, living wills and durable powers of attorney—aren't we ready for euthanasia?

Frank A. Oski, "Opting Out," *The Nation*, vol. 258, January 24, 1994, pp. 77–78. Copyright © 1994 by *The Nation* Magazine/The Nation Company, Inc. Reproduced by permission.

Passive euthanasia is the removal of an artificial barrier to death, thus allowing nature to take its course, and is generally accepted as a humane medical practice. Active euthanasia involves affirmative action to induce death before nature can take its course in the terminally ill patient who requests it, and should be viewed as the ultimate act of humanity.

The recent debate on active euthanasia began when Kevorkian assisted in the suicide of three patients who had serious but not imminently fatal diseases. He developed a crude but effective suicide machine that allowed individuals to take their own lives in a painless and efficient fashion. After his first patient died, first-degree murder charges were brought against him but were subsequently dismissed. Kevorkian continued the practice and on November 30 [1993] he was jailed. He staged a hunger strike to draw public attention to the issue, and after some time in jail, and promising that further attempts at assisted suicide would not occur, he was released on bail.

Proponents of Euthanasia Predate Kevorkian

The advocates of "get Kevorkian and teach him a lesson" seem ignorant of the history of the U.S. movement to legalize euthanasia, which long predates the good doctor. It began in 1906 when the Ohio legislature referred a bill to its Committee on Medical Jurisprudence, which proposed the legalization of active voluntary euthanasia. The bill was rejected by a vote of 78 to 22. Subsequent attempts to legalize the practice occurred in Nebraska, New York and in [1994] in the state of Washington, where approximately 223,000 citizens signed a peitition calling for an amendment to the state's living will law. Broad support was generated for the idea, but voters defeated Initiative 119 by a margin of 54 percent to 46 percent.

Today most states prohibit assisted suicide; Illinois, Ohio and Michigan call it murder. But even so, prosecution of those who have helped a person to die is unusual. It is not surprising that there is so much variation from state to state, because doctors themselves do not agree on the morality of active euthanasia.

Terminally Ill Patients Need Options

If you become terminally ill, what can you do? Will you attempt to find a friend or physician who can help spare you the pain of a lingering death? Can physicians serve in their traditional role of healer and still assist suicides? Twelve physicians examined this issue in the *New England Journal of Medicine*. Ten of them concluded that doctors should be able to provide hopelessly ill patients who believe their condition is intolerable with the knowledge and the means to commit suicide. The group also conlcuded that it would be lawful, under certain circumstances, for physicians to assist patients in ending their lives.

Dr. Timothy Quill offers a more specific prescription. With several colleagues, he has proposed guidelines for physicians who find assisted suicide morally acceptable that include: 1) the patient must, of his or her own initiative, clearly and repeatedly request to die rather than continue suffering; 2) the patient's judgement must not be distorted; 3) the patient must have a condition that is incurable and associated with severe, unrelenting, intolerate suffering; 4) the physician must insure that the patient's suffering and the request are not the result of inadequate comfort care; and 5) consultation with another doctor who is experienced in comfort care should take place.

Dying patients need more than prescriptions for mind-numbing narcotics. They need a personal guide and counselor to assist them on their last journey. Opponents of euthanasia argue that this is just the edge of the slippery slope to widespread abuse. They point to the atrocities of Nazi Germany and to the myriad examples of doctors who have acted unethically in Russia, Chile, South Africa and Japan. The debate has begun, thanks to Dr. Kevorkian. The American public must participate in this debate; after all, it is our lives that are at stake. Jailing the debaters, like Kevorkian, will do nothing to hasten the resolution of this problem.

"In Kevorkian's ideal world, doctors would decide when your life is no longer worth living."

Media Coverage Ignores Kevorkian's Dark Side

Michael Betzold

Michael Betzold is a Michigan-based writer who has researched and written about Dr. Jack Kevorkian's campaign for assisted suicide. His book on the subject is titled Appointment with Dr. Death.

In the following excerpt Betzold makes the case that Kevorkian has been obsessed with death—in particular, with finding uses for dead bodies—since he began his medical career. The media ignore this "mad scientist" aspect of the retired pathologist's campaign, according to Betzold, because it sympathizes with his aims. In addition, Kevorkian's attorney, Geoffrey Fieger, has been successful in hiding from the public Kevorkian's dark past and unusual ideas. The lawyer has been able, with the help of willing media, to present the issue of euthanasia as an issue of patient control. This obscures Kevorkian's true goals, which Betzold believes will give doctors control over patients.

Jack Kevorkian doesn't equivocate about his mission in life. It is to pioneer radical change in the way human beings die. In his writings and statements, Kevorkian advocates a society that allows euthanasia for the dying, the disabled, the mentally

Michael Betzold, "The Selling of Doctor Death: How Jack Kevorkian Became a National Hero," *The New Republic*, vol. 216, no. 21, May 26, 1997, pp. 22–28. Copyright © 1997 by The New Republic, Inc. Reproduced by permission of *The New Republic*.

ill, infants with birth defects and comatose adults; and he sanctions experiments prior to their death and organ harvesting. He envisions a global system of death on demand run by doctors who operate without oversight from government or ethicists. His "potential candidates for the humane killing known as euthanasia" are many. As Kevorkian describes in his book *Prescription: Medicide: The Goodness of Planned Death*, they include those afflicted by "the end stage of incurable disease, crippling deformity, or severe trauma," people with "intense anxiety or psychic torture inflicted by self or others," and those "who decide that they must die because of" their "religious or philosophical tenets or inflexible personal convictions," as well as "fetuses, infants, minor children, and every human being incapable of giving direct or informed consent."

In 1993, a *Time* interviewer asked Kevorkian: "How do you decide whom to help? Does the patient have to suffer from a life-threatening illness?"

"No, of course not," replied Kevorkian. "And it doesn't have to be painful, as with quadriplegia. But your life quality has to be nil."

"And who decides that?"

"That's up to physicians, and nobody can gainsay what doctors say."

And Kevorkian wants doctors to manipulate deaths for scientific gain. "It would be a unique privilege in the most emphatic sense to be able to experiment on a doomed human being," Kevorkian has written. "Help[ing] suffering or doomed patients kill themselves," he says, is "merely the first step . . . what I find most satisfying is the prospect of making possible the performance of invaluable experiments." What sort of experiments would Kevorkian like to perform? "No aim could be too remote, too silly, too simple, too absurd; and no experiment too outlandish." . . .

Media Coverage Favors Kevorkian

Kevorkian has never renounced his vision. Yet the public portrayal of Kevorkian does not do justice to the alarming scope of his aims. The media, who have given Kevorkian much attention since he attended his first death in June 1990, usually depict him in euphemistic and flattering terms, as a freedom fighter, a pioneer of the "right to die."

"Polls show a majority of Americans support Kevorkian's efforts to help the terminally ill end lives of suffering," intoned [reporter] Stone Phillips on [the television show] "Dateline NBC" [in 1996]. It was the kind of misleading statement typical in coverage of Kevorkian. In fact many of Kevorkian's customers have not been terminally ill. A few have been depressed. Autopsies have shown a few clients had no detectable physical ailments. Kevorkian's practice has been amateurish, his safeguards shoddy. But facts about his clients and his methods are consistently sanitized for public consumption.

Over the past seven years [1991–1997], the Kevorkian cure has dispatched at least forty-five customers (the count is hard to figure, since Kevorkian does not acknowledge all the deaths in which he participates). The idea that, in his work, Kevorkian is fighting for our "right not to suffer" and our freedom to die is generally unchallenged. Rarely is it pointed out that Americans already enjoy a "right not to suffer" (one can refuse medical treatment) and a right to die (one can commit suicide). And even more rarely do reporters examine Kevorkian's cases to determine who controls these experiments in death—the doomed human being or the experimenter.

Journalists legitimize Kevorkian's activities as medical practice by calling him a doctor, without mentioning that his Michigan medical license was revoked in 1991 and that the only remedies he "prescribes" are poisons. They call his customers "patients," though people come to him to be put away, not cured. They call the deaths he engineers "assisted suicides," though no one really knows how his customers die.

The selling of Kevorkian and the distortion of his program constitute not simply a failure of a lazy, sloppy and biased press, but also a public relations triumph for a man who has spent [from 1991 to 1997] as Kevorkian's attorney, image consultant, press secretary and all-around handler, Geoffrey Fieger. In that time, Fieger has transformed his client from media devil to media darling. In this, his biggest asset has been *The New York Times*, which has set a favorable tone for international coverage by using a cheerleader for Fieger and Kevorkian as its lead reporter on the story.

At War with Death

In Kevorkian's ideal world, doctors would decide when your life is no longer worth living. As the baby-boomer population enters its declining years, and as pressures to ration health-care services increase, such a prospect might seem frightening. But most Americans don't see Kevorkian's work in those terms, because they see what Fieger and the media have told them to see.

Dr. Howard Brody, a medical ethicist at Michigan State University, wonders about this. "If Dr. Kevorkian went on TV and said: My mission, my crusade is 'All power to the doctors,' I don't think he'd get the time of day from anybody," Brody told me. "And yet when he says, 'I'm Doctor Death,' everybody says: Great, this guy's a savior."...

Kevorkian is at war with death. He believes science should triumph over death, not compromise with it. He scorns both traditional religions and New Age spiritualism for seeing anything of value in death. He sees nothing in death but defeat. When I asked him what he believes happens after a person dies, he replied: "You rot." The rotting frustrates him. He's always sought ways to extract medical benefits for humanity out of what he sees as useless individual deaths. It is this impulse, rather than simply the desire to help people die, that motivates Kevorkian; in caricature, he would be, I think, more properly seen as a mad scientist than a ghoul. . . .

Kevorkian's first court appearances were not a public relations success. Representing himself, Kevorkian tried to submit a twenty-page statement of "testimony" from Aristotle, Pliny the Elder, Thomas Jefferson and Albert Einstein. The judge didn't allow it. Obviously, Kevorkian needed not only a lawyer, but a packager, a manager. But who could package and manage a megalomaniac?

Creating a Hero

Geoffrey Fieger once bragged to me that he was "the Ty Cobb" of attorneys. Like the legendary baseball bully, Fieger believes in winning by any means necessary. He is a lawyer of the showman school—he majored in drama in college before becoming a medical malpractice attorney—and he is relentless in court. He has won huge awards by portraying clients as victims of doctors.

Kevorkian hired Fieger in August 1990. Since then, Fieger has helped Kevorkian win three acquittals. He's also shaped the public Kevorkian into a heroic figure. Fieger has made the Kevorkian story irresistible to reporters, a circus in constant flux, with himself as the ringmaster. He knows what the media want: the crude, the sensational, the outrageous. Once, Fieger pinned a clown nose on the prosecutor's photo. He has called state appeals judges "squirrels and rats and lizards and mollusks.". . .

Fieger has staged Kevorkian's deaths as psychodramas that play on popular fears of disease and dying. In Fieger's depiction, Kevorkian's clients are always in excruciating and unceasing pain, their lives are always undignified, their prospects are always gruesome. Television news viewers and newspaper readers see in Fieger's depiction of "the suffering patient" their parents, their spouses, themselves. How could anyone object to putting these poor people out of their misery?

And Fieger can put the issue of assisted suicide in ideological terms that most journalists respond to with reflexive favor. The issue, Fieger insists, is not about doctors gaining more power to decide who can die, it is about civil rights. Fieger screams that authorities are intruding into our sick beds, making criminals of dying people. The government and the religious right, he contends, are usurping a fundamental freedom, the "right not to suffer." He once admitted to me that the "right not to suffer" would be a legal artifice and that "there's nothing constitutionally defective about a law outlawing assisted suicide . . . but certain things must be protected against lunatics."

"Lunatics" are behind any criticism of Kevorkian's work, Fieger asserts. Although in fact it is proponents of assisted suicide who are proposing radical change. Fieger argues that his opponents are the extremists, attempting "to impose a theocracy on the United States," as Fieger told me. In Boston [in 1996], Fieger told a cheering audience: "This is the civil rights issue. And if you don't stand up and say, 'Hell no, you Christian Coalition, you right-wingers, I own my own life. I own my life,' then you ain't free." When a lone critic challenged him, Fieger shot back: "If you and people like you are populating heaven, then I want to go to hell."

CHAPTER 2

Upholding the State's Right to Ban Assisted Suicide

Case Overview

Washington v. Glucksberg (1997)

Washington State passed a ban on assisted suicide in its Natural Death Act of 1979. The law completely forbade a physician-assisted suicide. Dr. Harold Glucksberg, along with a group of Washington right-to-die activists and terminally ill patients challenged the law in the federal courts. They argued that the law was too broad and it interfered with terminally ill patients' "liberty interests" under the due process clause of the Fourteenth Amendment. Moreover the state had no rational interest, as required by the Fourteenth Amendment, in preventing the suicide of those who were soon to die.

The first judge to hear the case, in the district court for western Washington, agreed with the Glucksberg group that the prohibition on assisted suicide was unconstitutional. Washington State appealed the ruling, but the United States Court of Appeals for the Ninth Circuit also held the law to be unconstitutional. The court of appeals ruled that bodily autonomy and the person's liberty interests outweigh the state interest in preventing suicide, an interest that was vastly decreased in the case of the terminally ill.

The court of appeals' decision relied on two Supreme Court precedents, the case of *Cruzan v. Director, Missouri Department of Health* (1990) and the case of *Planned Parenthood v. Casey* (1992). In *Cruzan*, one of the major right-to-die cases, the Court recognized the right of a patient to refuse medical treatment. In *Casey*, the Court reaffirmed the right to be free of government regulation that encroached on bodily autonomy. Taken together, reasoned the circuit court, these rulings implied that Washington State had no right to impose a complete ban on assisted suicide.

The Supreme Court heard the *Glucksberg* case in January 1997, along with a similar case (*Quill v. Vacco*), and rendered its decision in June of that year. It overruled the court of appeals, declaring that Washington did have a legitimate interest in banning assisted suicide. It rejected the argument that *Cruzan* and *Casey* implied a right to assisted suicide, noting that *Cruzan* dealt with a right not to have medical treatment forced on one's person, while *Casey* simply did not address the issue of assisted suicide.

On the practical level, the state had a legitimate fear that assisted suicide could lead to involuntary euthanasia, as it had in the Netherlands. Siding with tradition, the Court noted that current laws in most states were against assisted suicide, as was current medical practice. On the constitutional level, the Court noted that a vigorous debate over end-of-life policies was being conducted in the various states of the union. The Court's opinion expressed a reluctance to substitute its own judgment in the place of democratic debate on matters such as assisted suicide.

> *"Step by step, the state has acknowledged that terminally ill persons are entitled in a whole variety of circumstances to hasten their deaths."*

Ninth Circuit Court's Ruling: Interests of the Terminally Ill Outweigh the State's Interest in Preventing Suicide

Stephen Reinhardt

Stephen Reinhardt was appointed to the United States Court of Appeals for the Ninth Circuit in 1979. Prior to his appointment he served in the air force and practiced as a private attorney in Los Angeles.

In 1996, the United States Court of Appeals for the Ninth Circuit struck down as unconstitutional the Washington State law banning suicide as unconstitutional. The court of appeals objected to the law because it failed to balance the "liberty interest" of the terminally ill against the state's interest in preserving life. In the following excerpt, Judge Reinhardt focuses specifically on the state's interest in preventing suicide. He acknowledges that the state has such an interest, but argues that in the case of the terminally ill, the patient's right to die supersedes the state's interest. Moreover, there has been a step-by-step progression in this area, with states slowly acknowledging the rights of patients to refuse treatment or even to receive pain medication that may hasten death, he asserts. Finally, Reinhardt holds that the progress of medical science makes it impossible for the state to draw a

Stephen Reinhardt, 9th Circuit Court opinion, *Washington v. Glucksberg*, May 28, 1996.

valid distinction between active suicide and passive "letting die"; therefore, the Washington State law banning assisted suicide is an unconstitutional infringement on individual liberty.

While the state's general commitment to the preservation of life clearly encompasses the prevention of suicide, the state has an even more particular interest in deterring the taking of one's own life. The fact that neither Washington nor any other state currently bans suicide, or attempted suicide, does not mean that the state does not have a valid and important interest in preventing or discouraging that act.

Suicide Prevention Is the State's Primary Interest

During the course of this litigation, the state has relied on its interest in the prevention of suicide as its primary justification for its statute. The state points to statistics concerning the rate of suicide among various age groups, particularly the young. As the state notes, in 1991, suicide was the second leading cause of death after accidents for the age groups 15–19, 20–24, and 25–34 and one of the top five causes of death for age groups 35–44 and 45–54. These figures are indeed distressing.

Although suicide by teenagers and young adults is especially tragic, the state has a clear interest in preventing anyone, no matter what age, from taking his own life in a fit of desperation, depression, or loneliness or as a result of any other problem, physical or psychological, which can be significantly ameliorated. Studies show that many suicides are committed by people who are suffering from treatable mental disorders. Most if not all states provide for the involuntary commitment of such persons if they are likely to physically harm themselves. For similar reasons, at least a dozen states allow the use of nondeadly force to prevent suicide attempts.

While the state has a legitimate interest in preventing suicides in general, that interest, like the state's interest in preserving life, is substantially diminished in the case of terminally ill, competent adults who wish to die. One of the heartaches of suicide is the senseless loss of a life ended prematurely. In the case of a terminally ill adult who ends his life in the final stages of an incurable and painful degenerative disease, in order to avoid debilitating pain and a humiliating death, the decision to commit suicide is not senseless, and death does not come too early. Unlike [examples such as] "the depressed twenty-one year old, the romantically devastated twenty-eight year old, the alcoholic forty-year old," or many others who may be inclined to commit suicide, a terminally ill competent adult cannot be cured. While some people who contemplate suicide can be restored to a state of physical and mental well-being, terminally ill adults who wish to die can only be maintained in a debilitated and deteriorating state, unable to enjoy the presence of family or friends. Not only is the state's interest in preventing such individuals from hastening their deaths of comparatively little weight, but its insistence on frustrating their wishes seems cruel indeed. As Kent said in [Shakespeare's play] *King Lear*, when signs of life were seen in the dying monarch:

> Vex not his ghost: O! let him pass; he hate him That would upon the rack of this tough world Stretch him out longer.

State Interest Is Subordinate to Individual Liberty

The state has explicitly recognized that its interests are frequently insufficient to override the wishes of competent, terminally ill adult patients who desire to bring their lives to an end with the assistance of a physician. Step by step, the state has acknowledged that terminally ill persons are entitled in a whole variety of circumstances to hasten their deaths and that in such cases their physicians may assist in the process. Until relatively recently, while physicians routinely helped patients to hasten their deaths, they did so discreetly because almost all such assistance was illegal. However, beginning about twenty years ago a series of dramatic changes took place. Each provoked the type of division and debate that surrounds the issue before us today. Each time the state's interests were ultimately subordinated to the liberty interests of the individual, in part as a result of legal actions and in part as a result of a growing recognition by the medical community and society at large that a more enlightened approach was essential.

The first major breakthrough occurred when the terminally ill were permitted to reject medical treatment. The line was drawn initially at extraordinary medical treatment because the distinction between ordinary and extraordinary treatment appeared to some to offer the courts an objective, scientific standard that would enable them to recognize the right to refuse certain medical treatment without also recognizing a right to suicide or euthanasia. That distinction, however, quickly proved unworkable, and after a while, terminally ill patients were allowed to reject both extraordinary and ordinary treatment. For a while, rejection of treatment, often through "do not resuscitate" orders, was permitted, but termination was not. This dividing line, which rested on the illusory distinction between commission and omission (or active and passive), also appeared for a short time to offer a natural point of repose for doctors, patients and the law. However, it, too, quickly proved untenable, and ultimately patients were allowed both to refuse and to terminate medical treatment, ordinary as well as extraordinary. Today, many states also allow the terminally ill to order their physicians to discontinue not just traditional medical treatment but the artificial provision of life-sustaining food and water, thus permitting the patients to die by self-starvation. Equally important, today, doctors are generally permitted to administer death-inducing medication, as long as they can point to a concomitant pain-relieving purpose.

In light of these drastic changes regarding acceptable medical practices, opponents of physician-assisted suicide must now explain precisely what it is about the physician's conduct in assisted suicide cases that distinguishes it from the conduct that the state has explicitly authorized. The state responds by urging that physician-assisted suicide is different in kind, not degree, from the type of physician-life-ending conduct that is now authorized, for three separate reasons. It argues that "assisted suicide": 1) requires doctors to play an active role; 2) causes deaths that would not result from the patient's underlying disease; and 3) requires doctors to provide the causal agent of patients' deaths.

Current Practice Tantamount to Assisted Suicide

The distinctions suggested by the state do not individually or collectively serve to distinguish the medical practices society currently accepts. The first distinction—the line between commission and omission—is a distinction without a difference now that patients are permitted not only to decline all medical treatment, but to instruct their doctors to terminate whatever treatment, artificial or otherwise, they are receiving. In disconnecting a respirator, or authorizing its disconnection, a doctor is unquestionably committing an act; he is taking an active role in bringing about the patient's death. In fact, there can be no doubt that in such instances the doctor intends that, as the result of his action, the patient will die an earlier death than he otherwise would.

Similarly, drawing a distinction on the basis of whether the patient's death results from an underlying disease no longer has any legitimacy. While the distinction may once have seemed tenable, at least from a metaphysical standpoint, it was not based on a valid or practical legal foundation and was therefore quickly abandoned. When Nancy Cruzan's feeding and hydration tube was removed, she did not die of an underlying disease.[1] Rather, she was allowed to starve to death. In fact, Ms. Cruzan was not even terminally ill at the time, but had a life expectancy of 30 years. Similarly, when a doctor provides a conscious patient with medication to ease his discomfort while he starves himself to death—a practice that is not only legal but has been urged as an alternative to assisted suicide—the patient does not die of any underlying ailment. To the contrary, the doctor is helping the patient end his life by providing medication that makes it possible for the patient to achieve suicide by starvation.

Pain Medications Hasten Death

Nor is the state's third and final distinction valid. Contrary to the state's assertion, given current medical practices and current medical ethics, it is not possible to distinguish prohibited from permissible medical conduct on the basis of whether the medication provided by the doctor will cause the patient's death. As part of the tradition of administering comfort care, doctors have been supplying the causal agent of patients' deaths for decades. Physicians routinely and openly provide medication to terminally ill patients with the knowledge that it will have a "double effect"—reduce the patient's pain and hasten his death. Such medical treatment is accepted by the medical profession as meeting its highest ethical standards. It commonly takes the form of putting a patient on an intravenous morphine drip, with full knowledge that, while such treatment will alleviate his pain, it will also indubitably hasten his death. There can be no doubt, therefore, that the actual cause of the patient's death is the drug administered by the physician or by a person acting under his supervision or direction. Thus, the causation argument is simply "another bridge crossed" in the journey to vindicate the liberty interests

1. Nancy Cruzan suffered brain damage in a 1983 accident. In 1990, after seven years in a vegetative state and several court battles, she was disconnected from her feeding tube and died.

of the terminally ill, and the state's third distinction has no more force than the other two.

The Next Judicial Step

We acknowledge that in some respects a recognition of the legitimacy of physician-assisted suicide would constitute an additional step beyond what the courts have previously approved. We also acknowledge that judicial acceptance of physician-assisted suicide would cause many sincere persons with strong moral or religious convictions great distress. Nevertheless, we do not believe that the state's interest in preventing that additional step is significantly greater than its interest in preventing the other forms of life-ending medical conduct that doctors now engage in regularly. More specifically, we see little, if any, difference for constitutional or ethical purposes between providing medication with a double effect and providing medication with a single effect, as long as one of the known effects in each case is to hasten the end of the patient's life. Similarly, we see no ethical or constitutionally cognizable difference between a doctor's pulling the plug on a respirator and his prescribing drugs which will permit a terminally ill patient to end his own life. In fact, some might argue that pulling the plug is a more culpable and aggressive act on the doctor's part and provides more reason for criminal prosecution. To us, what matters most is that the death of the patient is the intended result as surely in one case as in the other. In sum, we find the state's interests in preventing suicide do not make its interests substantially stronger here than in cases involving other forms of death-hastening medical intervention. To the extent that a difference exists, we conclude that it is one of degree and not of kind.

> "Legal physician assisted suicide could make it more difficult for the State to protect depressed or mentally ill persons."

The Supreme Court's Decision: The State Has a Legitimate Interest in Preventing Assisted Suicide

William H. Rehnquist

In this excerpt from the Supreme Court's decision in Washington v. Glucksberg *(1997), chief justice William H. Rehnquist makes the case that the traditions of the United States do not support a fundamental right to die. On the other hand, the state (in this case Washington but implying any state in the union) has an interest in protecting the lives of its citizens. Rehnquist relies on research into assisted suicide in the Netherlands that shows that the legalization of the practice in that country has led to the euthanizing of citizens without clear consent. American state governments may choose not to risk such a situation and thus are entitled to ban assisted suicide. Rehnquist notes that there are ongoing debates in the various states over assisted suicide; he believes that the public should have the right to conduct the debate without the Supreme Court deciding the issue.*

William H. Rehnquist was the chief justice of the United States from 1986 until his death in 2005. He was appointed to the Supreme Court by President Richard Nixon in 1972.

William H. Rehnquist, majority opinion, *Washington v. Glucksberg*, January 26, 1997.

The history of the law's treatment of assisted suicide in this country has been and continues to be one of the rejection of nearly all efforts to permit it. That being the case, our decisions lead us to conclude that the asserted "right" to assistance in committing suicide is not a fundamental liberty interest protected by the Due Process Clause [of the Fourteenth Amendment]. The Constitution also requires, however, that Washington's assisted suicide ban be rationally related to legitimate government interests. This requirement is unquestionably met here. As the court below recognized, Washington's assisted suicide ban implicates a number of state interests.

An Unqualified Interest in Protecting Life

First, Washington has an "unqualified interest in the preservation of human life." The State's prohibition on assisted suicide, like all homicide laws, both reflects and advances its commitment to this interest. This interest is symbolic and aspirational as well as practical. [As the New York State Commission on Life and the Law wrote:]

> "While suicide is no longer prohibited or penalized, the ban against assisted suicide and euthanasia shores up the notion of limits in human relationships. It reflects the gravity with which we view the decision to take one's own life or the life of another, and our reluctance to encourage or promote these decisions."

Respondents [Glucksberg and his pro-assisted-suicide group] admit that "[t]he State has a real interest in preserving the lives of those who can still contribute to society and enjoy life." The Court of Appeals also recognized Washington's interest in protecting life, but held that the "weight" of this interest depends on the "medical condition and the wishes of the person whose life is at stake." Washington, however, has rejected this sliding scale approach and, through its assisted suicide ban, insists that all persons' lives, from beginning to end, regardless of physical or mental condition, are under the full protection of the law. As we have previously affirmed [in *Cruzan v. Director, Missouri Dept. of Health* (1990)], the States "may properly decline to make judgments about the 'quality' of life that a particular individual may enjoy." This remains true, as *Cruzan* makes clear, even for those who are near death.

Relatedly, all admit that suicide is a serious public health problem, especially among persons in otherwise vulnerable groups. The State has an interest in preventing suicide, and in studying, identifying, and treating its causes.

Those who attempt suicide—terminally ill or not—often suffer from depression or other mental disorders. Research indicates, however, that many people who request physician assisted suicide withdraw that request if their depression and pain are treated. The New York Task Force, however, expressed its concern that, because depression is difficult to diagnose, physicians and medical professionals often fail to respond adequately to seriously ill patients' needs. Thus, legal physician assisted suicide could make it more difficult for the State to protect depressed or mentally ill persons, or those who are suffering from untreated pain, from suicidal impulses.

Protecting the Medical Profession

The State also has an interest in protecting the integrity and ethics of the medical profession. In contrast to the Court of Appeals' conclusion that "the integrity of the medical profession would [not] be threatened in any way by [physician assisted suicide]," the American Medical Association, like many other medical and physicians' groups, has concluded that "[p]hysician assisted suicide is fundamentally incompatible with the physician's role as healer." And physician assisted suicide could, it is argued, undermine the trust that is essential to the doctor-patient relationship by blurring the time-honored line between healing and harming.

Next, the State has an interest in protecting vulnerable groups—including the poor, the elderly, and disabled persons—from abuse, neglect, and mistakes. The Court of Appeals dismissed the State's concern that disadvantaged persons might be pressured into physician assisted suicide as "ludicrous on its face." We have recognized, however, the real risk of subtle coercion and undue influence in end of life situations. Similarly, the New York Task Force warned that "[l]egalizing physician assisted suicide would pose profound risks to many individuals who are ill and vulnerable. . . . The risk of harm is greatest for the many individuals in our society whose autonomy and well being are already compromised by poverty, lack of access to good medical care, advanced age, or membership in a stigmatized social group." If physician assisted suicide were permitted, many might resort to it to spare their families the substantial financial burden of end of life health care costs.

The State's interest here goes beyond protecting the vulnerable from coercion; it extends to protecting disabled and terminally ill people from prejudice, negative and inaccurate stereotypes, and "societal indifference." The State's assisted suicide ban reflects and reinforces its policy that the lives of terminally ill, disabled, and elderly people must be no less valued than the lives of the young and healthy, and that a seriously disabled person's suicidal impulses should be interpreted and treated the same way as anyone else's.

The Path to Euthanasia

Finally, the State may fear that permitting assisted suicide will start it down the path to voluntary and perhaps even involuntary euthanasia. The Court of Appeals struck down Washington's assisted suicide ban only "as applied to competent, terminally ill adults who wish to hasten their deaths by obtaining medication prescribed by their doctors." Washington insists, however, that the impact of the court's decision will not and cannot be so limited. If suicide is protected as a matter of constitutional right, it is argued, "every man and woman in the United States must enjoy it." The Court of Appeals' decision, and its expansive reasoning, provide ample support for the State's concerns. The court noted, for example, that the "decision of a duly appointed surrogate decision maker is for all legal purposes the decision of the patient himself," that "in some instances, the patient may be unable to self administer the drugs and . . . administration by the physician . . . may be the only way the patient may be able to receive them," and that not only physicians, but also family members and loved ones, will inevitably participate in assisting suicide. Thus, it turns out that what is couched as a limited right to "physician assisted suicide" is likely, in effect, a much broader license, Which could prove extremely difficult to police and contain. Washington's ban on assisting suicide prevents such erosion.

This concern is further supported by evidence about the practice of euthanasia in the Netherlands. The Dutch government's own study revealed that in 1990, there were 2,300 cases of voluntary euthanasia (defined as "the deliberate termination of another's life at his request"), 400 cases of assisted suicide, and more than 1,000 cases of euthanasia without an explicit request. In addition to these latter 1,000 cases, the study found an additional 4,941 cases where physicians administered lethal morphine overdoses without the patients' explicit consent. This study suggests that, despite the existence of various reporting procedures, euthanasia in the Netherlands has not been limited to competent, terminally ill adults who are enduring physical suffering, and that regulation of the practice may not have prevented abuses in cases involving vulnerable persons, including severely disabled neonates [newborn infants] and elderly persons suffering from dementia. The New York Task Force, citing the Dutch experience, observed that "assisted suicide and euthanasia are closely linked," and concluded that the "risk of . . . abuse is neither speculative nor distant." Washington, like most other States, reasonably ensures against this risk by banning, rather than regulating, assisting suicide.

Public Debate Should Continue

We need not weigh exactingly the relative strengths of these various interests. They are unquestionably important and legitimate, and Washington's ban on assisted suicide is at least reasonably related to their promotion and protection. We therefore hold that [Washington's prohibition of assisted suicide] does not violate the Fourteenth Amendment, either on its face or "as applied to competent, terminally ill adults who wish to hasten their deaths by obtaining medication prescribed by their doctors."

Throughout the Nation, Americans are engaged in an earnest and profound debate about the morality, legality, and practicality of physician assisted suicide. Our holding permits this debate to continue, as it should in a democratic society. The decision of the en banc [full bench] Court of Appeals is reversed, and the case is remanded for further proceedings consistent with this opinion.

> *"A condition-based rule in favor of assisted suicide would pour into the Constitution a poisonous concoction of warm-hearted, misguided pity and cold-hearted utilitarianism."*

Assisted Suicide Endangers States' Ability to Protect Life

Carl A. Anderson

Carl A. Anderson is the current chief executive officer of the Knights of Columbus, a Roman Catholic fraternal organization. In this excerpt from an amicus curiae *("friend of the court") brief, written when he was the public policy director for the organization, Anderson argues that a right to assisted suicide would be a dangerous departure from previous Supreme Court decisions. First, Anderson argues that the right to assisted suicide found by the U.S. Court of Appeals for the Ninth Circuit (in its decision in* Washington v. Glucksberg*) and the U.S. Court of Appeals for the Second Circuit (in the companion case* Quill v. Vacco*) does not promote liberty as understood by the framers of the Constitution. Second, Anderson raises the question of whether patients whose treatment is costly will be pressured to give up their right to life. By allowing the terminally ill to alienate—that is, to give up—their right to life, he believes the right to suicide will create a situation where the disabled and chronically ill are less protected than at present.*

Carl A. Anderson, amicus brief in *Washington v. Glucksberg* and *Quill v. Vacco*, November 12, 1996.

To deflect concerns about assisted suicide raised by persons with disabilities and members of other vulnerable populations, the Ninth and Second Circuits responded with assurances that suicide is a constitutional benefit. Based on the considerations addressed in the remainder of this brief, your Amici ["friends of the court"] disagree strongly.

In no other case has the Supreme Court been asked to license an individual to assist in the intentional destruction of life at the request of the victim. All other claims of personal freedom granted constitutional protection have related in some meaningful way to the individual's enjoyment of life and continued participation in society. Thus, the Supreme Court has "reject[ed] at the outset the notion that any grievous loss visited upon a person by the State is sufficient to invoke" a constitutional remedy. Whether an asserted interest to act free from government interference rises to the level of a constitutional right will depend on its "nature"—that is, its relation to the "'whole domain of social and economic fact,'" as well as on its connection to an individual's ability to "'engage in any of the common occupations of life.'"

Assisted Suicide Is Antithetical to Liberty

Conversely, a "right" or "liberty" to obtain suicide assistance would lack any relation to the capacity to exist, move freely, and form personal attachments in society; it would be entirely antithetical to such exercises of liberty. Assisted suicide accomplishes the purposeful destruction of life and, as a result, forever cuts the victim off from all ties to family, friends, and society. It thus fails to achieve any "benefit" of existence or social inclusion ascertainable under the Constitution.

The Ninth and Second Circuit [Courts of Appeal] attempted to graft assisted suicide to the outer branches of the right to accept or refuse medical treatment. They argued that if the Constitution recognizes a right to make medical decisions, then it should recognize the right to assisted suicide.

The courts thus contended that the personal and state interests at stake in treatment refusal and assisted suicide cases are indistinguishable, particularly with respect to their relationship to death.

On the contrary, the right to accept or refuse treatment differs significantly from an interest in suicide assistance precisely because treatment decisions can enable persons to "engage in the common occupations of life." Moreover, the constitutional strength of an interest in making treatment decisions diminishes as the risk of death increases, while the proposed interest in assisted suicide would increase in strength because its objective is death.

States Intervene to Protect Life

This Court [in *Whalen v. Roe* (1977)] has acknowledged the existence of a "right to decide independently, with the advice of [a] physician, to acquire and to use needed medication [i.e., essential to health]." Treatment may be necessary to prolong life, to alleviate pain, or to overcome any other maladies which might hinder an individual's capacity to work or to engage in social activities. These benefits undoubtedly comport with the Constitution's life-enhancing objectives.

In addition, this Court has recognized an interest "in avoiding the unwanted administration of ... drugs." This interest also relates to constitutional objectives by directly implicating the freedom to move about in society unimpeded by the intrusive restraint of a technological apparatus or the forced ingestion of pills or medication.

To the extent that a decision to accept or refuse treatment implicates hastened death, this Court has permitted the states to limit the decision maker's discretion. Thus, the states may "prohibit entirely the use of particular drugs" deemed dangerous to the patient's health and safety, and may consider such "dramatic consequences" as death when weighing the policy implications of refusing treatment. Far from endorsing in these cases any principle that would support the creation of a right to purposely cause death, the Court has permitted the states to circumscribe the right to accept or refuse treatment in direct proportion to the likelihood that death will result.

Death Is Not a Noble Objective

Fundamental rights are protected because they enable individuals to live freely and interact socially, even if at times their exercise involves personal risk. The rights to speak, vote, travel, refuse treatment, and so on, could be equated to assisted suicide only by irrebuttably imputing to the citizen who chooses to exercise them in risky situations an inherent desire to be harmed—and by falsely imputing to the Constitution's framers the intent to recognize death as simply another noble objective.

Instead, a constitutionally protected decision to purposely seek death would be unique among all other protected choices. It would embrace a lethal purpose, while the exercise of other rights merely tolerate certain residual and unavoidable risks. Its objective is death rather than life, and its exercise results in irreversible alienation rather than social participation. While the "recognition of any right creates the possibility of abuse," a constitutional policy favoring assisted suicide eliminates any contingency by endorsing what is itself a form of abuse. Indeed, the abuses of other freedoms—involving threats against life and self-expulsion from society—would frame the essence of this new right. The dangers its constitutional enshrinement would pose for persons with terminal conditions, other vulnerable populations, and society itself would be of a far greater magnitude than the risks created by the exercise of any other right.

While the assisted suicide claim before this Court ostensibly concerns individual rights, the Court must also consider the social consequences. In particular, constitutionalizing the right to seek to harm one's self with the assistance of others says just as much about the constitutional status of persons granted this right as it says about the right itself. Thus, the question is broader than "does the life-destroying right to assisted suicide share equal billing with other freedoms that are instead life-enhancing?" The inquiry must also focus on why the right to live of some persons should be slashed in value from an unalienable to an alienable constitutional interest.

The Ninth and Second Circuits tied the strength of one's right to live to one's proximity to death, thereby provoking a profound fear among many of those persons in society whose disabilities leave them with an already precarious hold on life. Every person with a disabling condition is already more intensely aware than most of life's contingent nature, even if his or her present condition is not certifiably terminal. Many persons with disabilities were disabled by accidents and thus have peered through the gates of death before medicine made survival possible. Many persons with disabilities rely on high tech interventions to survive, to breathe or to eat, and they are constantly reminded by the nature of their ongoing care that without proper treatment or care they would soon die. Many persons with disabilities depend on the assistance of family, friends, and professional caregivers and must orchestrate ever-shifting schedules simply to meet the minimum requirements of daily living. Some, like the actor Christopher Reeve [paralyzed in a horseback-riding accident] cannot function without substantial medical and personal assistance. Most are far less capable than a wealthy movie star of meeting the financial burdens of their care, however, and few enjoy the same public esteem. Most members of this class are unquestionably more vulnerable to discrimination and social alienation.

Assisted Suicide Makes the Disabled More Vulnerable

Many persons with disabilities exist in a state of "virtual terminality" because the frailty of their physical condition and the specter of death are so intimately woven together. In turn, a constitutional decision asserting that their right to live is constitutionally disposable makes them "virtual aliens" because their most fundamental right—the protection of life—would hang only by the single thread of their own resolve to keep it. They will be left far less secure against both internal and external pressures to give away this right to the unjust advantage of others.

In the end, a condition-based rule in favor of assisted suicide would pour into the Constitution a poisonous concoction of warm-hearted, misguided pity and cold-hearted utilitarianism. The question of "whether we as a society are willing to excuse the terminally ill for deciding that their lives are no longer worth living" would be mixed inextricably with the question of whether assisted suicide should serve as a means "for housecleaning, cost-cutting and burden shifting; a way to get rid of those whose lives we deem worthless" (*Compassion in Dying*, [*v. State of Washington*, 1996]). Who stands to benefit most from a constitutional policy by which the right to live of vulnerable persons is reduced to an alienable interest? Is it the person with a terminal condition bent on suicide regardless of what the Constitution holds, or is it a cost-conscious society seeking more ways to ration its generosity?

"The Washington statute . . . deprives these patients of the ability to exercise control over the manner of their death."

The Personal Autonomy of the Terminally Ill Outweighs States' Interest in Protecting Life

Janet Benshoof and Kathryn Kolbert

Washington v. Glucksberg *involved many of the same issues as abortion rights cases; therefore it was of interest to reproductive rights groups. The following is an excerpt from an amicus curiae ("friend of the court") brief, which is a letter from a third party—usually an organization—that supports one side or the other in a particular case. Writing on behalf of the Center for Reproductive Law and Policy, attorneys Janet Benshoof and Kathryn Kolbert argue that a right to assisted suicide can be derived from the right to bodily integrity found in a series of Supreme Court decisions. In particular the Supreme Court's decision in* Cruzan v. Director, Missouri Department of Health *(1990) and the New Jersey Supreme Court's decision* In re: Karen Ann Quinlan *(1976)—both of which granted a "right to die" based on personal autonomy and bodily integrity—establish that patients have a right to control their own bodies.*

According to Benshoof and Kolbert, Washington State's complete prohibition of assisted suicide does not respect these well-established precedents. The state's attempt to draw a distinction between the withdrawal of treatment and active assisted suicide

Janet Benshoof and Kathryn Kolbert, amicus brief of the Center for Reproductive Law and Policy (in the case of *Washington v. Glucksberg*), 1996.

is irrelevant because the constitutional right of the terminally ill to bodily autonomy trumps state interest in protecting life. While states can establish regulations to ensure against abuse of assisted suicide, Benshoof and Kolbert argue, they cannot establish blanket prohibitions against the practice.

Janet Benshoof is founder and past president of the Center for Reproductive Law and Policy. Kathryn Kolbert has been recognized as one of the one hundred most influential lawyers in America by the National Law Journal. *She has argued in front of the United States Supreme Court in reproductive rights cases.*

In an effort to distinguish the protections *Cruzan* affords to individuals to hasten their death, the State of Washington argues that its absolute prohibition does not implicate a protected liberty interest because it does not compel anyone to use life-sustaining treatment, but rather, prohibits terminally ill persons from choosing to take medication to hasten death.

But it is well-established that the Constitution's protections of the body are not limited to halting governmental intrusions into the body. The Constitution also guarantees decisional autonomy concerning one's body, affording individuals both the right to seek and the right to decline medical treatment. Indeed, this Court's cases concerning the Constitution's protection of bodily integrity have long recognized a close connection between bodily integrity and personal autonomy. The Constitution protects against governmental intrusion into one's body in order to protect the individual's freedom to make decisions concerning her body. As Justice [Sandra Day] O'Connor explained in *Cruzan*, this Court has deemed "state incursions into the body repugnant to the interests protected by the Due Process Clause," precisely because "our notions of liberty are inextricably intertwined with our idea of physical freedom and self-determination."

Freedom to Choose Medical Treatment

Individual self-determination over one's body is not limited to the freedom to reject medical treatment. Bodily integrity and autonomy, if it is to mean anything, must include a patient's freedom to choose a course of medical treatment. After all, "[n]o right is held more sacred . . . than the right of every individual to the possession and control of his person, free from all restraint and interference from others. . . ."

Similarly, by prohibiting terminally ill patients from making the deeply personal decision to take medication to hasten death, the Washington statute at issue here deprives these patients of the ability to exercise control over the manner of their death, their bodies, and [in the words of Justice O'Connor] "the course of [their] own medical treatment," often forcing them to endure anguish and pain until they die. Indeed, for terminally ill patients, the prospect of death defines their existence and circumscribes the exercise of their life choices. Because much of their lives have become focused on preparation for death, the decision about whether to hasten death is often one of the few defining decisions that terminally ill persons may make concerning their lives.

Furthermore, Washington's absolute prohibition on medical assistance to hasten death leaves terminally ill patients with only two choices: to remain on treatment regimes, which often require them to endure intense anguish and pain, and prolong their life, or to refuse treatment, thereby causing them even more severe pain. To many this dilemma leaves terminally ill patients feeling "captive of the machinery" required for their treatment, "burdening [their] . . . liberty interests as much as any direct state coercion." By forcing plaintiffs to undergo these state-mandated harms when their physicians could provide medication to relieve their pain, once and for all, the statutes here deprive them of a substantial liberty interest.

Rights Are Not Defined by Historical Practice

Washington [State] also argues that the Constitution affords no protection to the decision to seek medication to hasten death because of the long history of state statutes banning assisted suicide. But this Court has long rejected the view that the Due Process Clause protects only those practices historically permitted by the states. The right to use contraceptives, the right to choose abortion, the right to marry a person of another race, and the right to be free of state-mandated segregated schooling are among the rights protected by the Due Process Clause despite a long history of statutes denying these rights.

As this Court explained . . . [in *Harper v. Virginia State Board of Elections* (1996)], "we have never been confined to historic notions of equality, any more than we have restricted due process to a fixed catalogue of what was at a given time deemed to be the limits of fundamental rights." "The very purpose of a Bill of Rights was to withdraw certain subjects from the vicissitudes of political controversy, to place them beyond the reach of majorities and officials and to establish them as legal principles to be applied by the courts" [*West Virginia State Bd. of Educ. v. Barnette* (1943)]. The Constitution's protections "may not be submitted to a vote; they depend on the outcome of no elections."

Moreover, as this Court has often recognized, relying exclusively on what the states have legislated in determining the scope of the Constitution's protections would imperil numerous constitutional freedoms recognized by this Court's decisions. As . . . [prior] cases demonstrate, there are sound reasons for this refusal to place reliance on historical practice in determining the scope of the liberty protected by the Due Process Clause. "A prime part of the history of our Constitution . . . is the story of the extension of constitutional rights and protections to people once ignored and excluded." . . .

A reviewing court must weigh both the nature and character of the liberty deprivation and the asserted state interests in determining the validity of the state's regulation. The rigor of the Court's review of the state interests depends on the burden imposed by the statute. Where the individual's liberty interest is substantial, the state must come forward with a correspondingly substantial justification, requiring the court to consider the possibility of less intrusive alternatives.

Ban on Assisted Suicide Is a Deprivation of Liberty

There can be no question that the statutory prohibitions here deprive terminally ill persons of a substantial liberty interest. These statutes bar, without exception, all terminally ill persons from seeking medication to hasten death, preventing them from making the deeply personal decision to hasten death, and depriving them of the power to exercise control over their bodies in an effort to avoid the intense and brutal pain caused by their illness.

In its brief to this Court, Washington offers two rationales for its total prohibition on this substantial liberty interest: the protection of human life and the protection of vulnerable patients from mistake and abuse. Neither of these important interests, however, supports the complete prohibition at issue here. Moreover, these interests do not explain or justify the lines drawn by the Washington legislature. . . .

This Court's precedents concerning "personal autonomy and bodily integrity" have long recognized that a "State's interest in the protection of life falls short of justifying any plenary override of individual liberty claims." [*Planned Parenthood v. Casey* (1992), citing *Cruzan*.] This must certainly be the case where, as here, the state seeks to further this interest by preventing terminally ill patients from ending their life in dignity, in their own way and on their own terms. Ever since the New Jersey Supreme Court's landmark decision in *In re*

Quinlan [1976], courts have refused to force terminally ill patients "to endure the unendurable, only to vegetate a few measurable months with no realistic possibility of returning to any semblance of cognitive and sapient life." Instead, as in *Quinlan* the state's interest in preserving life "weakens and the individual's right to privacy grows as the degree of bodily invasion increases and the prognosis dims." Where, as here, the life of a terminally ill person is nearing its end and that person is suffering from intense pain, that individual's substantial liberty interest in bodily integrity surely must "overcome the State interest."

Moreover, Washington itself recognizes, in the context of a patient's request to terminate life-sustaining treatment, that the interest in preserving life must give way to the individual's right to control his body and die with dignity. By court decision and statute, Washington law permits a terminally ill patient to hasten death by refusing life-sustaining treatment or by directing physicians to remove such treatment. These statutes and court decisions, which recognize that the state's interest in the preservation of life cannot justify overriding the wishes of a terminally ill person who seeks to hasten his death by terminating life-sustaining treatment, powerfully undermine Washington's claim that a total prohibition is necessary to further its legitimate interest in preserving life. State regulatory efforts, like those upheld by this Court in *Cruzan*, can strike the proper balance between the individual's freedom to control his or her body and die in a dignified manner and the state interest in preserving life. Here too, Washington's statutes and cases recognize that, for terminally ill patients, decisions concerning whether to die with dignity are [in the words of this Court] "too vital to be banned."

Manner of Death Is Constitutionally Irrelevant

In an effort to distinguish this body of law, Washington and their amici argue that there are differences between terminating life-sustaining treatment and prescribing medication: in one instance, the physician lets the patient die; in the other, the medication causes the patient's death. This is a distinction, but not a relevant one for constitutional line-drawing. It does not explain why the state's interest in preserving life must give way to the right of a terminally ill patient to hasten death by terminating or refusing life-sustaining treatment, but not the right of a terminally ill person to seek medication to hasten death. In both instances, the patient's decision inevitably results in death. If the state's interest in life does not support a complete ban on terminating life-sustaining treatment, it is difficult to understand why that same interest supports the ban here simply because death occurs in a different manner. . . .

Termination of life-sustaining treatment raises exactly the same problems concerning mistake and abuse as the prescription of medication to hasten death. In both cases, doctors may abuse their authority and pressure terminally ill persons to hasten their deaths. Washington has not explained why the pressures exerted by physicians in this context—both subtle and otherwise—are any different when a physician withdraws a patient's life-sustaining treatment. In the face of this silence, the untested assumption that procedural safeguards would be unworkable is wholly unreasonable and cannot justify the absolute prohibition here.

Regulations Can Ensure Against Involuntary Euthanasia

The United States[1], in an effort to distinguish the two practices, argues that a patient's choice to hasten death often reflects inadequate treatment for the patient's pain, not a true desire to hasten death. The total ban, they argue, should be upheld because of a "very significant risk that persons with

1. That is, the United States Department of Justice, which argued in support of the Washington State ban on assisted suicide.

treatable depression and pain will be allowed to commit suicide." Even if this is an "overriding interest," far less intrusive
measures could allay this concern without the need for the flat
prohibition imposed by the state. Before permitting physicians
to prescribe medication to hasten death, states have broad discretion to enact measures to ensure that a patient's decision is
truly voluntary, and not the result of inadequate pain management. The State has failed to explain why these less intrusive measures would not adequately serve this interest. Indeed,
the protocols used by Compassion in Dying[2] illustrate some
of the procedural safeguards available to ensure voluntariness.

In view of the plaintiffs' strong liberty interest and the
state's inability to convincingly explain why a prohibition is
necessary here, but not in the context of the termination of
life-sustaining treatment, these statutes must be declared unconstitutional as applied to plaintiffs.

---

2. An organization that promotes assisted suicide and that was a respondent in this case.
   It has published guidelines to help avoid abuse of the practice.

> *"Assisted suicide is a choice about self determination, and terminally ill patients deserve the chance to make an individual decision about how and when to die."*

The *Glucksberg* Case Has Resulted in Better End-of-Life Care

Philip King

With an aging population and better medical technology, a larger percentage of today's population will face prolonged illness that leads to death than ever before. Doctors and nurses have not traditionally focused on the challenges of helping the terminally ill; most of their training has been in helping patients who will recover to functioning health.

In the following excerpt, Philip King outlines the implications of Washington v. Glucksberg *(1997) for health-care providers. Some doctors have already been involved in assisted suicide, but King notes that the case has been a "wake-up call" for the healing professions. A more open discussion of end-of-life care has been the result. Medical schools are offering courses to students in palliative care—the area of medicine focusing on pain relief for people who will not recover from their illness. King believes that developments in pain control and end-of-life care will give terminal patients more options; they will no longer face the choice between unbearable pain or clandestine euthanasia.*

Philip King, "*Washington v. Glucksberg*: Influence of the Court in Care of the Terminally Ill and Physician Assisted Suicide," *Journal of Law and Health*, vol. 15, no. 2, summer 2000, pp. 271–301. Copyright © 2000 Cleveland-Marshall College of Law. Reproduced by permission.

Philip King is a graduate of Cleveland-Marshall College of Law. Now in private practice, he is also a city councilman in Chardon, Ohio. His interest in medical issues arises from service as a certified paramedic with the Chardon Fire Department.

Glucksberg [1997] contains some significant implications for the medical care of terminally ill patients and the relief of their pain and suffering. The right-to-end-life issue before the Court in *Glucksberg* identified the importance of palliative care for the terminally ill patient. A report by the Institute of Medicine at the National Academy of Science identified the under-treatment of pain and the use of ineffectual and intrusive medical procedures that may prolong suffering as major problems in end-of-life care. Terminally ill patients are concerned about loss of personal autonomy, loss of control of bodily functions, and the control of severe pain. Pain at the end of life is the most common reason people seek medical care. The treatment of pain is often neglected in medical education and in care for the patient. The assisted suicide issue has made end-of-life care the focal point in the decision making process of how one dies.

Physicians Currently Practice Assisted Suicide

Assisted suicide has been practiced by physicians without statutory authorization or medical protection. In April 1998, the Massachusetts Medical Society published the results of a 1996 national survey involving 3102 physicians in ten specialty firms throughout the country. The survey reported that a substantial number of physicians in the United States had received requests for assisted suicide, and that about six percent complied with the request at least one time. The study demonstrated that region of practice, religion, and specialty influenced a physician's participation in assisted death. The report suggested that the open debate in the states of California, Oregon, and Washington may account for the higher frequency of assisted suicide requests and physician compliance with such requests in these states.

The study found that a majority of the patients who requested assisted suicide would have met regulatory safeguards similar to a those in Oregon's statute authorizing assisted suicide. The study discovered that in a majority of the cases, hospitalized patients who received a lethal injection had less than twenty-four hours to live and were experiencing severe discomfort or pain. The study suggested that by delaying treatment of the patients' pain symptoms, the physician could protect against an accusation that he or she was intending to hasten death. The report recommended additional research to evaluate the possibility that better access to palliative care might eliminate some of the requests for physician assisted suicides. The survey also noted that the demand for assisted suicide, and a corresponding compliance by a doctor, might differ in communities where palliative care is easily accessible, suggesting fewer requests where palliative care is readily available. In *Glucksberg*, the Supreme Court also vocalized recognition of these circumstances, while suggesting that the legislature was the appropriate body to address the palliative care issue.

The use of lethal injection seemed to be the method of choice by physicians for patients having less that twenty-four hours to live and were experiencing severe discomfort and pain. The report suggested that additional research was necessary because the study was conducted when palliative care education was not available and the provision of end-of-life care was inconsistent throughout the country. The attitudes and choices of patients and physicians might change when palliative care becomes readily available and the needs of the patient become a larger factor in the medical treatment plan. The report also stated that current proposals for assisted suicide guidelines would bear little relation to the clinical circumstances involving physician care for the terminally ill patients. Current data indicates that physicians are inadequately trained to assess and manage the complex symptoms of pain that are commonly related to a patient's request for suicide. The appropriate and aggressive use of pain-relieving drugs is recommended even if the use of the drug hastens death. There have been improvements in the sensitivity of the medical community in relating to the needs and desires of the dying patient. Physicians have a responsibility to undertake timely and adequate discussions with patients for agreement, not only about life-sustaining treatment, but also on how they want to be cared for in the terminal stages of life. The involvement of the physician in end-of-life care planning is deficient in part because of inadequate training provided to medical students. Consequently, practitioners may not sufficiently understand or value the role of the terminally ill patient in making decisions about terminal care issues.

Doctors Respond to Debate over Assisted Suicide

According to American Medical Association reports, only five of the 126 medical schools in the United States require a course that specifically concentrates on palliative care. Patients do not have confidence that the health care system will take care of the needs of a terminally ill patient; particularly with regard to the care necessary to deal with pain. Some health care providers have expressed that "there is no doubt that the debate and high degree of tolerance shown for assisted suicide has been a wake up call to the medical system."

While there is considerable support for the contention that the field of medicine has had a long track record of under-treating the pain of terminally ill patients, the health care community is beginning to respond to the public debate on assisted suicide. Pain control is now part of many specialty areas of medicine, and experts report that ninety-five percent of patients with intractable pain can experience relief without intolerable sedation. Patients with severe and intractable pain do not have to end their life, and palliative care opportunities offer the most crucial element in caring to the needs of the terminally ill patient. Under current guidelines for assisted suicide, the terminally ill patient is the only individual who is permitted the choice of ending his or her life.

The care of the dying patient is an art that not only prepares the patient to cope with the technology of the medical environment; it is an art of deliberately developing the circumstances that allow the patient to experience a peaceful death. The physician must balance the inadequate treatment of the dying patient with the intolerable use of aggressive life-sustaining procedures in order to achieve a level of care that maximizes the comfort and dignity of the dying patient.

Quality of Life Is the Utmost Goal

The humanness of death is not only a matter of avoiding pain and physical suffering, it is also about being consistent with the basic values of the patient. Patients fear and resent the experience of death which could be preceded by a period of dependency or deterioration. Consequently, the World Health Organization has endorsed palliative care as an integral component of a national health care policy. The World Health Organization has also taken the position that its member countries are not to consider the legalization of assisted suicide without having adequately addressed the need for pain relief and palliative care. There is considerable evidence which suggests that a request for assistance in suicide may mask an underlying need for pain relief.

The goal of palliative care is to relieve suffering and place the utmost importance on the quality of the patient's life. Palliative medicine focuses on improving the control of pain, and management of the symptoms of the disease, while at the same time addressing the psychological needs of patients and families facing a life-limiting illness. Palliative medicine attempts to influence how a patient dies. The terminally ill patient must be prescribed whatever is medically necessary to control pain.

According to the Massachusetts Medical Society, narcotics or other pain medications should be given in whatever dose and by whatever route is necessary for relief. It further advocates that it is morally appropriate to increase the dosage to levels needed even to the point where death is hastened, provided that the primary objective of the necessary treatment plan is to relieve pain. This result is commonly referred to as the double effect. The double effect occurs when a terminally ill patient, in consultation with a physician, chooses to receive major doses of pain-killing drugs under palliative care with knowledge that the treatment may, as a secondary effect, result in death. Physicians have continuously argued that there is a critical difference between the intent of a course of care that results in death secondary to the intent of the treatment of pain even when the death is foreseeable and the primary intent to assist in a suicide and the intent of administering a lethal injection purely because it is lethal. The American Medical Association Code of Ethics supports the role of the physician using an aggressive treatment plan for pain in a palliative care circumstance even when the foreseeable result could produce death.

More Training in End-of-Life Care

The practice of palliative health care is beginning to evolve; a recent survey by the Association of American Medical Colleges reported that 122 of 125 accredited medical schools offered end-of-life studies as part of required medical courses. Fifty of those schools offered separate elective courses focusing on caring for the dying patient. Health care professionals see that making physicians and nurses aware of end-of-life issues is just the first step. The second step is to increase awareness and opportunities in the hospital care setting.

The availability of palliative care provides for the relief of severe pain and symptom management for the terminally ill patient. The terminally ill patient considers assisted suicide only as a viable alternative to suffering severe pain during the final stages of life. The use of assisted suicide as a means of end-of-life care will be effectively reduced by improvements in palliative care options. The political debate on assisted suicide must focus on the needs of the terminally ill patient and the choices he or she must make to die with dignity and individual autonomy. Viewed from this perspective, the legal and medical community can address the palliative care needs, thereby the assisted suicide choice becomes a less desirable option in the care for terminally ill patients. Assisted suicide is a choice about self-determination, and terminally ill patients deserve the chance to make an individual decision about how and when to die.

CHAPTER 3

The Schiavo Case Highlights Divisions over the Right to Die

Case Overview

In re: The Guardianship of Theresa Marie Schiavo (2000)

In 1990 Theresa (Terri) Schiavo, a twenty-six-year-old married woman from St. Petersburg, Florida, fell into a coma. Her illness was caused by a chemical imbalance that caused her heart to stop. By the time she made it to the hospital, her brain was severely damaged due to lack of oxygen. After emergency treatment, she was diagnosed as being in a persistent vegetative state; her brain stem functioned to maintain a heartbeat and breathing, but she showed no response to external stimulus.

Terri's husband, Michael, initially hoped that Terri would recover. He pursued an aggressive course of treatments, including having her flown to California for experimental therapy. However, Terri showed no improvement. She was placed in a hospice, where she received basic care. The damage to her brain was so severe she could not swallow food or water. Accordingly, the feeding tube that had been inserted during her hospital treatment remained in place; she continued to receive nourishment and hydration via the tube.

In the meantime Michael Schiavo won malpratice settlements totaling $1 million from doctors who had been treating Terri for an eating disorder at the time of her collapse. With the money he set up a fund to pay for Terri's care. Though at first he was active in safeguarding Terri's well-being, after a period of time he ordered that she not be treated for infections and eventually indicated that he believed Terri would have wanted artificial feeding and hydration stopped. Terri's parents, the Schindlers, were concerned by these developments. They tried to remove Michael as Terri's guardian.

The case went to the Florida probate court in Pinellas County, where in 2000 Judge George W. Greer decided that "clear and convincing evidence" showed that Theresa Schiavo would not have wanted to be kept alive artificially under her present conditions. Florida does not require a written statement expressing the incapacitated person's desire to remove artificial life-sustaining treatment—including hydration and nourishment. Courts had the power to decide such cases based on what the patient had confided to friends and family before the accident. Michael's statements were backed up by those of his brother and sister-in-law, who testified that Terri had several times expressed a desire to be allowed to die in the case she was being kept alive by artificial means. The judge found this testimony credible and he agreed with Michael Schiavo that the feeding tube could be removed.

The Schindlers appealed the ruling in three separate instances, but each time the Florida courts sided with Michael Schiavo. Attempts to involve the state legislature and governor Jeb Bush were ruled unconstitutional by the Florida Supreme Court. The federal courts refused to review the case initially; when an act of Congress made it possible for the Schindlers to appeal to federal courts, these courts—including the Supreme Court—refused to hear the case. The Schindlers had exhausted all options; Terri's feeding tube was removed on March 18, 2005, and she died of dehydration on March 31. The Schiavo case was important on several levels. It served to underline sharp divisions in the United States between supporters of the right to life and those who prize "individual autonomy." The divisions were made more obvious by a religious factor; Americans who are religious tended to favor the Schindlers' position, while less-religious people favored Michael Schiavo's decision to let his wife die. The case also raised constitutional issues, particularly over the separation of powers when Florida's legislature and governor tried to intervene in the case after a judicial decision had been made.

> "If I ever go like that just let me go.
> Don't leave me there. I don't want to
> be kept alive on a machine."

The Trial Court's Ruling: Convincing Evidence Shows Terri Schiavo Would Have Wanted to Die

George W. Greer

The Pinellas County, Florida, probate court was the first court to rule in the Theresa (Terri) Schiavo case. Previous Florida court cases had resulted in a three-part test in deciding whether an incapacitated person would want medical treatment withdrawn. The judge, George W. Greer, had to decide whether the incapacitated person's guardian, in this case her husband, Michael Schiavo, had faithfully followed oral declarations of the patient, was reasonably sure that the patient would never recover competency, and obeyed any conditions or limitations that the patient had placed on the desire to have medical care withdrawn.

Based on the testimony of Michael Schiavo, his brother, and the brother's wife, Judge Greer decided that Terri Schiavo had indeed expressed the desire to have medical treatment withdrawn if she became permanently incapacitated. Judge Greer also took testimony from a health-care professional who noted that Terri Schiavo's supposed comments to her brother- and sister-in-law were typical of such statements. With medical experts agreeing that there was no reasonable hope for recovery and what he regarded as convincing evidence of Terri Schiavo's

George W. Greer, opinion in *In re: The Guardianship of Theresa Marie Schiavo*, February 11, 2000.

wishes, Judge Greer ordered that Michael Schiavo could order the removal of the feeding tube that sustained Terri's life.

George W. Greer is a judge in the Pinellas County circuit court. He is legally blind, a condition some believe gives him empathy with disabled people who come before his court.

Michael Schiavo testified as to a few discussions he had with his wife concerning life support. The Guardian Ad Litem felt that this testimony standing alone would not rise to clear and convincing evidence of her intent. The court is not required to rule on this issue since it does have the benefit of the testimony of his brother and sister-in-law. As with the witness called by the Respondents [the Schindlers], the court had the testimony of the brother and sister-in-law [Scott and Joan Schiavo] transcribed so that the court would not be hamstrung by relying upon its notes. The court has reviewed the testimony of Scott Schiavo and Joan Schiavo and finds nothing contained therein to be unreliable. The court notes that neither of these witnesses appeared to have shaded his or her testimony or even attempt to exclude unfavorable comments or points regarding those discussions. They were not impeached on cross-examination. Argument is made as to why they waited so long to step forward but their explanations are worthy of belief. The testimony of Ms. Beverly Tyler, Executive Director of Georgia Health Discoveries, clearly establishes that the expressions made by Terri Schiavo to these witnesses are those type of expressions made in those types of situations as would be expected by people in this country in that age group at that time. They (statements) reflect underlying values of independence, quality of life, not to be a burden and so forth. "Hooked to a machine" means they do not want life artificially extended when there is not hope of improvement.

Medical Issues

Turning to the medical issues of the case, the court finds beyond all doubt that Theresa Marie Schiavo is in a persistent vegetative state [as] the same is defined by Florida [law] per the specific testimony of Dr. James Barnhill and corroborated by Dr. Vincent Gambone. The medical evidence before this court conclusively establishes that she has no hope of ever regaining consciousness and therefore capacity, and that without the feeding tube she will die in seven to fourteen days. The unrebutted medical testimony before this court is that such death would be painless. The film offered into evidence by Respondents does nothing to change these medical opinions which are supported by the CAT scans in evidence. Mrs. Schindler has testified as [to] her perceptions regarding her daughter and the court is not unmindful that perceptions may become reality to the person having them. But the overwhelming credible evidence is that Terri Schiavo has been totally unresponsive since lapsing into the coma almost ten years ago, that her movements are reflexive and predicated on brain stem activity alone, that she suffers from severe structural brain damage and to a large extent her brain has been replaced by spinal fluid, that with the exception of one witness whom the court finds to be so biased as to lack credibility, her movements are occasional and totally consistent with the testimony of the expert medical witnesses. The testimony of Dr. Barnhill establishes that Terri Schiavo's reflex actions such as breathing and movement shows merely that her brain stem and spinal cord are intact.

Legal Requirements

The controlling legal authority in this area is a case which arose in St. Petersburg. A little over nine years ago, the Florida Supreme Court rendered its opinion in a case in which the State of Florida was opposing the withdrawal of feeding tubes. In that case Estelle Browning had a living will and the issue was essentially whether or not an incapacitated person possessed the same right of privacy to withhold or withdraw life-supporting medical treatment as did a competent person. The

Florida Supreme Court began with the premise that everyone has a fundamental right to the sole control of his or her person. They cited [a] 1914 New York decision in holding that an integral component of this right of privacy is the "right to make choices pertaining to one's health, including the right to refuse unwanted medical treatment." The court also found that all life-support measures would be similarly treated and found no significant legal distinction between artificial means of life support. Citing its earlier decision of *John F. Kennedy Memorial Hospital, Inc.* vs *Bludworth* (1984) the Court held that the constitutionally protected right to choose or reject medical treatment was not diminished by virtue of physical or mental incapacity or incompetence. Citing the lower court, the Florida Supreme Court agreed that it was "important for the surrogate decisionmaker to fully appreciate that he or she makes the decision which the patient would personally choose" and that in Florida "we have adopted a concept of 'substituted judgment,'" and "one does not exercise another's right of self-determination or fulfil that person's right of privacy by making a decision which the state, the family or public opinion would prefer."

The Florida Supreme Court set forth a three-pronged test which the surrogate (in this case the Petitioner/Guardian) must pursue in exercising the patient's right of privacy. The surrogate must satisfy the following conditions:

1) The surrogate must be satisfied that the patient executed any document knowingly, willingly and without undue influence and that the evidence of the patient's oral declaration is reliable;

2) The surrogate must be assured that the patient does not have a reasonable probability of recovering competency so that the right could be exercised directly by the patient; and

3) The surrogate must take care to assure that any limitations or conditions expressed either orally or in the written declaration have been carefully considered and satisfied.

The Florida Supreme Court established the clear and convincing test as a requirement and further held that when "the only evidence of intent is an oral declaration, the accuracy and reliability of the declarant's oral expression of intent may be challenged."

Applying the Test

The court is called upon to apply the law as set forth in *Guardianship of Estelle M. Browning* [1990] to the facts of this case. This is the issue before the court. All of the other collateral issues such as how much was raised in the fund-raising activities, the quality of the marriage between Michael and Terri Schiavo, who owes whom between Michael Schiavo and Mr. and Mrs. Schindler, Mr. and Mrs. Schindler's access or lack of access to medical information concerning their daughter, motives regarding the estate of Terri Schiavo if deceased, and the beliefs of family and friends concerning end-of-life decisions are truly not relevant to the issue which the court must decide. That issue is set forth in the three-pronged test established by the Florida Supreme Court in the *Browning* decision. The court must decide whether or not there is clear and convincing evidence that Theresa Marie Schiavo made reliable oral declarations which would support what her surrogate (Petitioner/Guardian) now wishes to do. The court has previously found that the second part of that test, i.e., the patient does not have a reasonable probability of recovering competency, is without doubt satisfied by the evidence.

There are some comments or statements made by Terri Schiavo which the court does not feel are germane to this decision. The court does not feel that statements made by her at the age of 11 or 12 years truly reflect upon her intention regarding the situation at hand. Additionally, the court does not feel that her statements directed toward others and situations involving others would have the same weight as comments or statements regarding herself if personally placed in those same situations. Into the former category the court places statements regarding Karen Ann Quinlan [an earlier similar case] and the infant child of the friend of Joan Schiavo. The court finds that those statements are more reflective of what Terri Schiavo would do in a similar situation for someone else.

Clear and Convincing Evidence

The court does find that Terri Schiavo did make statements which are creditable and reliable, with regard to her intention given the situation at hand. Initially, there is no question that Terri Schiavo does not pose a burden financially to anyone and this would appear to be a safe assumption for the foreseeable future. However, the court notes that the term "burden" is not restricted solely to dollars and cents since one can also be a burden to others emotionally and physically. Statements which Terri Schiavo made which do support the relief sought by her surrogate (Petitioner/Guardian) include statements to him prompted by her grandmother being in intensive care that if she was ever a burden she would not want to live like that. Additionally, statements made to Michael Schiavo which were prompted by something on television regarding people on life support that she would not want to live like that also reflect her intention in this particular situation. Also the statements she made in the presence of Scott Schiavo at the funeral luncheon for his grandmother that "if I ever go like that just let me go. Don't leave me there. I don't want to be kept alive on a machine." and to Joan Schiavo following a television movie in which a man following an accident was in a coma to the effect that she wanted it stated in her will that she would want the tubes and everything taken out if that ever happened to her are likewise reflective of this intent. The court specifically finds that these statements are Terri Schiavo's oral declarations concerning her intention as to what she would want done under the present circumstances and the testimony regarding such oral declarations is reliable, is creditable and rises to the level of clear and convincing evidence to this court.

Those statements above noted contain no limitations or conditions. However, as Ms. Tyler noted when she testified as to quality of life being the primary criteria in artificial life support matters, Americans want to "try it for awhile" but they do not wish to live on it with no hope of improvement. That implicit condition has long since been satisfied in this case. Therefore, based upon the above and foregoing findings of fact and conclusions of law, it is

ORDERED AND ADJUDGED that the Petition for Authorization to Discontinue Artificial Life Support of Michael Schiavo, Guardian of the Person of Theresa Marie Schiavo, an incapacitated person, be and the same is hereby **GRANTED** and Petitioner/Guardian is hereby authorized to proceed with the discontinuance of said artificial life support for Theresa Marie Schiavo.

"Our hearts can fully comprehend the grief so fully demonstrated by Theresa's family members on this record. But our hearts are not the law."

The Florida Supreme Court's Decision: The Rule of Law Must Prevail in Right-to-Die Cases

Barbara J. Pariente

After losing their first trial in 2000, Terri Schiavo's parents, the Schindlers, pursued several appeals. These were all turned down, either by the original trial court judge, George W. Greer, or by Florida's Second District Court of Appeals. Their case generated publicity, however, and the Florida legislature attempted to step in to aid their quest to have Michael Schiavo removed as Terri's guardian.

The legislature passed a law in October 2003 that would allow governor Jeb Bush to place a stay, or suspension, on the removal of Terri Schiavo's feeding tube. When the governor did in fact prohibit the removal of the tube, Michael Schiavo took the case to the Florida Supreme Court. In the following excerpt from its ruling, Chief Justice Barbara J. Pariente holds that the legislature and governor's actions constitute a violation of the constitutional principle of separation of powers. The Schiavo case was adjudicated by a competent judge who followed existing Florida law. It was appealed through normal procedures and the original ruling was upheld. The legislature and governor endangered con-

Barbara J. Pariente, opinion in *Jeb Bush v. Michael Schiavo*, 2004.

stitutional democracy by stepping in after this process simply be-cause they did not like the outcome of the case. While the court expressed sympathy with the Schindlers, it stressed that law should rule rather than emotion and that the rule of law upheld the decision ordering the removal of the feeding tube.

Barbara J. Pariente was appointed chief justice of the Florida Supreme Court in 2004, where she had served as associate justice since 1997.

On October 21, 2003, the Legislature enacted chapter 2003-418 [of the Laws of Florida], the Governor signed the Act into law, and the Governor issued executive order No. 03-201 to stay the continued withholding of nutrition and hydration from Theresa [Schiavo]. The nutrition and hydration tube was reinserted pursuant to the Governor's executive order.

On the same day, Michael Schiavo brought the action for declaratory judgment in the circuit court. Relying on undisputed facts and legal argument, the circuit court entered a final summary judgment on May 6, 2004, in favor of Michael Schiavo, finding the Act unconstitutional both on its face and as applied to Theresa. Specifically, the circuit court found that chapter 2003-418 was unconstitutional on its face as an unlawful delegation of legislative authority and as a violation of the right to privacy, and unconstitutional as applied because it allowed the Governor to encroach upon the judicial power and to retroactively abolish Theresa's vested right to privacy.

Separation of Powers

We begin our discussion by emphasizing that our task in this case is to review the constitutionality of chapter 2003-418, not to reexamine the guardianship court's orders directing the removal of Theresa's nutrition and hydration tube, or to review the Second District's numerous decisions in the guardianship case. Although we recognize that the parties continue to dispute the findings made in the prior proceedings, these proceedings are relevant to our decision only to the extent that they occurred and resulted in a final judgment directing the withdrawal of life-prolonging procedures. . . .

Chapter 2003-418 allowed the Governor to issue a stay to prevent the withholding of nutrition and hydration from a patient. . . . Under the fifteen-day sunset provision, the Governor's authority to issue the stay expired on November 5, 2003. The Governor's authority to lift the stay continues indefinitely.

The cornerstone of American democracy known as separation of powers recognizes three separate branches of government—the executive, the legislative, and the judicial—each with its own powers and responsibilities. In Florida, the constitutional doctrine has been expressly codified in article II, section 3 of the Florida Constitution, which not only divides state government into three branches but also expressly prohibits one branch from exercising the powers of the other two branches:

> Branches of Government.—The powers of the state government shall be divided into legislative, executive and judicial branches. No person belonging to one branch shall exercise any powers appertaining to either of the other branches unless expressly provided herein. "This Court . . . has traditionally applied a strict separation of powers doctrine," and has explained that this doctrine "encompasses two fundamental prohibitions. The first is that no branch may encroach upon the powers of another. The second is that no branch may delegate to another branch its constitutionally assigned power." . . .

Encroachment on the Judicial Branch

We begin by addressing the argument that, as applied to Theresa Schiavo, the Act encroaches on the power and authority of the judicial branch. More than 140 years ago this Court explained the foundation of Florida's express separation of powers provision:

> The framers of the Constitution of Florida, doubtless, had in mind the omnipotent power often exercised by the British Parliament, the exercise of judicial power by the Legislature in those States where there are no written Constitutions restraining them, when they wisely prohibited the exercise of such powers in our State. . . .

Similarly, the framers of the United States Constitution recognized the need to establish a judiciary independent of the legislative branch. Indeed, the desire to prevent Congress from using its power to interfere with the judgments of the courts was one of the primary motivations for the separation of powers established at this nation's founding. . . .

Under the express separation of powers provision in our state constitution, "the judiciary is a coequal branch of the Florida government vested with the sole authority to exercise the judicial power," and "the legislature cannot, short of constitutional amendment, reallocate the balance of power expressly delineated in the constitution among the three coequal branches."

As the United States Supreme Court has explained, the power of the judiciary is "not merely to rule on cases, but to *decide* them, subject to review only by superior courts" and "[h]aving achieved finality . . . a judicial decision becomes the last word of the judicial department with regard to a particular case or controversy." Moreover, "purely judicial acts . . . are not subject to review as to their accuracy by the Governor."

Limits on Review of Judiciary

In *Advisory Opinion*, the Governor asked the Court whether he had the "constitutional authority to review the judicial accuracy and propriety of [a judge] and to suspend him from office if it does not appear . . . that the Judge has exercised proper judicial discretion and wisdom." The Court agreed that the Governor had the authority to suspend a judge on the grounds of incompetency "if the physical or mental incompetency is established and determined within the Judicial Branch by a court of competent jurisdiction." However, the Court held that the Governor did not have the power to "review the judicial discretion and wisdom of a . . . Judge while he is engaged in the judicial process.". . .

In this case, the undisputed facts show that the guardianship court authorized Michael to proceed with the discontinuance of Theresa's life support after the issue was fully litigated in a proceeding in which the Schindlers were afforded the opportunity to present evidence on all issues. This order as well as the order denying the Schindlers' motion for relief from judgment were affirmed on direct appeal. The Schindlers sought review in this Court, which was denied. Thereafter, the tube was removed. Subsequently, pursuant to the Governor's executive order, the nutrition and hydration tube was reinserted. Thus, the Act, as applied in this case, resulted in an executive order that effectively reversed a properly rendered final judgment and thereby constituted an unconstitutional encroachment on the power that has been reserved for the independent judiciary. . . .

Under procedures enacted by the Legislature, effective both before the passage of the Act and after its fifteen-day effective period expired, circuit courts are charged with adjudicating issues regarding incompetent individuals. The trial courts of this State are called upon to make many of the most difficult decisions facing society. In proceedings under chapter 765, Florida Statutes (2003), these decisions literally affect the lives or deaths of patients. The trial courts also handle other weighty decisions affecting the welfare of children such as termination of parental rights and child custody. When the prescribed procedures are followed according to our roles of court and the governing statutes, a final judgment is issued, and all post-judgment procedures are followed, it is without question an invasion of the authority of the judicial branch for the Legislature to pass a law that allows the executive branch to interfere with the final judicial determination in a case. That is precisely what occurred here and for that reason the Act is unconstitutional as applied to Theresa Schiavo. . . .

Rule of Law Must Prevail

We recognize that the tragic circumstances underlying this case make it difficult to put emotions aside and focus solely on the legal issue presented. We are not insensitive to the struggle that all members of Theresa's family have endured since she fell unconscious in 1990. However, we are a nation of laws and we must govern our decisions by the rule of law and not by our own emotions. Our hearts can fully comprehend the grief so fully demonstrated by Theresa's family members on this record. But our hearts are not the law. What is in the Constitution always must prevail over emotion. Our oaths as judges require that this principle is our polestar, and it alone.

As the Second District noted in one of the multiple appeals in this case, we "are called upon to make a collective, objective decision concerning a question of law. Each of us, however, has our own family, our own loved ones, our own children. . . . But in the end, this case is not about the aspirations that loving parents have for their children." Rather, as our decision today makes clear, this case is about maintaining the integrity of a constitutional system of government with three independent and coequal branches, none of which can either encroach upon the powers of another branch or improperly delegate its own responsibilities.

The continuing vitality of our system of separation of powers precludes the other two branches from nullifying the judicial branch's final orders. If the Legislature with the assent of the Governor can do what was attempted here, the judicial branch would be subordinated to the final directive of the other branches. Also subordinated would be the rights of individuals, including the well established privacy right to self determination. No court judgment could ever be considered truly final and no constitutional right truly secure, because the precedent of this case would hold to the contrary. Vested rights could be stripped away based on popular clamor. The essential core of what the Founding Fathers sought to change from their experience with English rule would be lost, especially their belief that our courts exist precisely to preserve the rights of individuals, even when doing so is contrary to popular will.

The trial court's decision regarding Theresa Schiavo was made in accordance with the procedures and protections set forth by the judicial branch and in accordance with the statutes passed by the Legislature in effect at that time. That decision is final and the Legislature's attempt to alter that final adjudication is unconstitutional as applied to Theresa Schiavo.

> *"The current, generally accepted applications to terminal illness or persistent vegetative state define artificial feeding as artificial life support that may be withheld or withdrawn."*

Florida Courts Followed the Law in a Difficult Case

Jay Wolfson

Jay Wolfson is a professor of public health at the University of South Florida. He served as Terri Schiavo's court-appointed guardian (guardian ad litem*) during the court proceedings involving Michael Schiavo and the Schindlers, Terri's family.*

In the following excerpt from a report submitted to Governor Jeb Bush, Wolfson explores some of the wider societal issues involved in the case. Wolfson notes that laws concerning the right to refuse medical treatment were revised recently in response to aging populations and changing ideas about personal autonomy. Laws vary from state to state; most states require some sort of written expression of the desire to be taken off life support in the event of permanent incapacitation. However, this issue was debated thoroughly in the Florida legislature, and in 1999 a law was passed that allowed guardians to substitute their own judgments in the event that the incapacitated person had clearly expressed his or her wishes prior to the accident or injury. Wolfson believes that there is some risk of confusing family wishes with the patient's wishes with such a law, but given that such a law was in place, the Florida courts did a competent job in following it.

Jay Wolfson, "A Report to Governor Jeb Bush and the 6th Judicial Circuit in the Matter of Theresa Marie Schiavo," December 1, 2003. Reproduced by permission.

Our society is at a legal, political, biotechnological, bioethical and spiritual crossroad. Theresa Schiavo is alternately depicted as a living, loving person, capable of interacting at a level of cognition with her family and deserving of the right to continue to live—and as a tragically and profoundly brain damaged person, who earlier expressed a desire never to find herself in a circumstance analogous to waking up in a coffin—and being there forever. But she cannot speak to us now. So we must rely upon the auspices of good law and good medicine and the good intentions of those who marshal these arts in order to do our best to do the right thing well for Theresa Schiavo.

Changes in the Law

During the early 1970s the States began to revise their Probate Codes.[1] There were many reasons for this, including a rapidly aging population, larger numbers of aged persons in the population, people living longer, new and advancing medical technologies that enhanced, extended and affected life, and changing values and orientations about death, dying and the medical-decision processes. These matters have been seriously addressed through a combination of inquiries and actions by church leaders, legislators, medical scientists, and the courts, as all have sought to respond to emerging issues such as those in the [Karen Ann] Quinlan, [Nancy] Cruzan, [Estelle] Browning,[2] and now the Schiavo cases.

States cooperated with the federal Administration on Aging to address legislative and policy challenges surfacing around these matters. A particularly important topic related to medical technology and its use in the care, treatment and maintenance of patients, is when, who and by what means "artificial" life support and other medical interventions should or could be removed or never withheld in the first place.

1. Laws dealing with wills and estates.
2. These women were all subjects of major right-to-die cases.

Today, most states would afford an adult person the right to deny most health care treatments. But if the patient is a minor, unconscious, in a coma, in a vegetative state, or unable to communicate personal wishes and intentions, there are serious moral, ethical and legal questions that demanded attention. There had been inconsistencies, even within states, as to how decisions regarding termination or removal or withholding a procedure were made. There was also a long-standing, well-accepted recognition that the relationship between the patient and the physician—the sacred trust—served as the foundation for how and where and when many of these decisions would be made. Often, physicians, in consultation with family members and the patient have done what was deemed to be in the best interests of the patient, given the physician's medical opinion and the express, known or believed intentions of the patient.

Living Wills Gain Acceptance

To reduce ambiguities, many states began to encourage and accept written advance directives as the basis for decisions regarding end-of-life treatment. Living wills, durable powers of attorney for health care and health care surrogate documents, stating a person's explicit intentions regarding end-of-life care, became increasingly accepted and even formalized into the statutory framework of most states. A written expression was deemed to be an important element in this process to avoid the possibility of confusion or uncertainty with respect to a person's intention regarding their health and medical care.

Throughout the 1980s and 1990s, Florida lawmakers struggled with how they would provide individuals with the prerogatives for establishing their wishes regarding end-of-life decisions, while at the same time, protecting against perceived and actual abuses and assisted suicides. Among the most sensitive of issues in this regard has been the withdrawal of artificial life support in the form of nutrition and hydration. The idea of withholding or withdrawing these has created significant debates within and across religious, philosophical and political groups and interests. But the topic has been addressed at great lengths by each of these groups, and there is surprising consensus in principle and even in practice.

The current, generally accepted applications to terminal illness or persistent vegetative state define artificial feeding as artificial life support that may be withheld or withdrawn. In 1989, the Florida Legislature permitted the withdrawal of artificial nutrition and hydration under very specific circumstances. In 1999, following extensive bipartisan efforts, life-prolonging procedures were redefined as "any medical procedure, treatment, or intervention, including artificially provided sustenance and hydration, which sustains, restores, or supplants a spontaneous vital function." It is noteworthy that the general principle of artificial nutrition as artificial life support that may be removed in terminal and even vegetative state conditions is reflected in nearly all states' laws and within the guidelines of end-of-life care enunciated by the American [U.S.] Conference of Catholic Bishops and other religious denominations.

These general principles are in no way intended to encourage or condone suicide or assisted suicide. But they reflect the acceptance of artificial nutrition as artificial life support that may be withdrawn or withheld as a matter of public policy, when these decisions capture the intentions of the person and with the premise that people should not be required to remain "artificially alive," or to have their natural peaceful deaths postponed and prolonged if they would otherwise choose not to, and that they should be allowed to die with dignity, and return, if their beliefs so accommodate, to God.

Substituting Court Judgment

When written advance directives are not available, and the affected person is incompetent and unable to communicate, a decision to discontinue nutrition and hydration is especially challenging. But Florida law . . . as interpreted through *In re Guardianship of Browning* (1990), provide for a substituted judgment basis for such decisions and/or the presentation of clear and convincing evidence to demonstrate the intentions of the person.

It has been suggested that in the case of incapacitated persons, particularly those who have not expressed an advance directive, the "clear and convincing" evidence standard for establishing the intent to discontinue artificial life support is insufficient and incongruous. The insufficiency, it is argued, is because of the possibility of using information that is not accurate, complete or even honest. The incongruity is related to the "beyond a reasonable doubt" standard that serves as the basis for decisions to convict and then execute capital felons.

If persons unable to speak for themselves have decisions made on their behalf by guardians or family members, the potential for abuse, barring clear protections, could lead to a "slippery slope" of actions to terminate the lives of disabled and incompetent persons. And it is not difficult to imagine bad decisions being made in order to make life easier for a family or to avoid spending funds remaining in the estate on the maintenance of a person.

Risk of Confusing Intentions

There is, of course, the other side of that slippery slope, which would be to keep people in a situation they would never dream of: unable to die, unable to communicate, dependent for everything, and unaware, being maintained principally or entirely through state resources—and for reasons that may relate to guilt, fear, needs or wants of family members, rather than what the person's best wishes might otherwise have been.

And there is the chillingly practical, other public policy matter of the cost of maintaining persons diagnosed in persistent vegetative states and terminal conditions alive for potentially indefinite periods of time—at what inevitably becomes public expense. Here the "reasonable person" standard, with respect to how one would want to be treated were they in Theresa's shoes affects the discussion. This is not easy stuff, and should not be.

In withholding or withdrawing life support, or in keeping a person alive, there is the risk of transposing intentions and values. The reasoned, even substituted, judgment decisions of guardians or loved ones may be based upon either a "quality of life determination," or the desires of family members. This remains a risk in a system that does not require an explicit, advance directive.

Legal System Performed Well

A legal analysis of the tens of thousands of pages of documents in the case file, against the statutory legal guidelines and the supporting case law, leads the GAL [guardian *ad litem*] to conclude that all of the appropriate and proper elements of the law have been followed and met. The law has done its job well. The courts have carefully and diligently adhered to the prescribed civil processes and evidentiary guidelines, and have painfully and diligently applied the required tests in a reasonable, conscientious and professional manner. The disposition of the courts, four times reviewed at the appellate level, and once refused review by the Florida Supreme Court, has been that the trier of fact followed the law, did its job, adhered to the rules and rendered a decision that, while difficult and painful, was supported by the facts, the weight of the evidence and the law of Florida.

> *"If the person is dying and all the nutrition and hydration is doing is prolonging death ... you might, in fact, have an obligation to stop that."*

Religion Is Influential in the Public's View of End-of-Life Issues

Joe Feuerherd

Many of those most opposed to the withdrawal of food and hydration from Terri Schiavo had strong religious convictions. In addition, Terri's family, the Schindlers, were devout Catholics strongly committed to the church's doctrine on right-to-life issues. These facts added to the intensity of the controversy in the case.

In the following article Joe Feuerherd, a writer for the National Catholic Reporter, *examines the views of Catholic clergy and health-care professionals regarding Schiavo before her death. Their views reflect a variety of thoughts on the matter. While Pope John Paul II believed that withholding food and water was tantamount to euthanasia, there is disagreement on whether this was official church teaching. Catholic bishops and theologians in the United States were divided on the issue. Although "there should be a presumption in favor of providing nutrition and hydration to all patients," wrote the bishops in a June 2001 statement, such a treatment should not involve "undue burdens" to the patient. The ethical difficulty, according to the experts inter-*

Joe Feuerherd, "Schiavo Case Highlights Divisions in Catholic Views on Treatment," *National Catholic Reporter*, vol. 41, April 1, 2005, pp. 5–6. Copyright © The National Catholic Reporter Publishing Company, 115 E. Armour Blvd., Kansas City, MO 64111. All rights reserved. Reproduced by permission of *National Catholic Reporter*, www.nat cath.org.

viewed by Feuerherd, is in deciding what exactly is an undue burden and who can decide these matters for incapacitated patients like Terri Schiavo.

Medically, Florida courts have accepted the determination that [Theresa (Terri)] Schiavo is in a "persistent vegetative state"—unaware of the world, unable to interact with those around her, and unlikely to improve. Others, including Schiavo's parents, contend that she may be in a "minimally conscious state"—aware to some degree of her environment, capable of limited interaction, and a candidate for therapeutic treatment that could yield tangible benefits.

Experts on Both Sides

"You've got competent medical experts lined up on both sides," said Dr. John Kilner, president of The Center for Bioethics and Human Dignity, Bannockburn, Ill.

And Schiavo's wishes? Florida courts have sided with Schiavo's husband, Michael, who says that prior to Terri's February 1990 incapacitation, she told him that she would not wish to continue to live if she found herself in such circumstances. But Michael Schiavo, say others, is hopelessly compromised—with both financial conflicts (he benefited from a malpractice award related to Terri's care) and personal interests (he is involved in a relationship with another woman who is the mother of his two children).

"You can't help but wonder about his motives," said Russell B. Connors, assistant professor of theology at Minnesota's College of St. Catherine.

"In the absence of an advance directive, there's commonly an ordering of who is in the best position to act in [the patient's] best interests and it's normal and natural that the spouse would be at the top of the list because the spouse has a unique relational commitment to that person," said Kilner. But in the Schiavo case, "virtually anyone would be in a better position [to carry out that role] than her husband."

Despite disputes over the nature of Terri Schiavo's condition and her intentions, the law has spoken and the gastric tube that provided her nourishment has been removed.

Does Catholic teaching allow for such a course of action? It depends, once again, on both the individual circumstances and the individual answering the question.

Ordinary vs. Extraordinary Medical Treatment

Though the terms are often misunderstood, traditional Catholic teaching distinguishes between "extraordinary" and "ordinary" means of medical treatment. "Extraordinary" doesn't necessarily mean cutting edge. Instead it relates to the burdens (physical, financial, familial) and benefits (such as extended life) that a particular treatment or procedure might entail. Depending on the circumstances, treatment with an antibiotic could be considered "extraordinary," while use of a ventilator to allow breathing may be "ordinary." Generally speaking, Catholics are free to forgo "extraordinary" treatment and obligated to accept "ordinary" treatment.

As the U.S. bishops said in June 2001, "A person may forgo extraordinary or disproportionate means of preserving life. Disproportionate means are those that in the patient's judgment do not offer a reasonable hope of benefit or entail an excessive burden, or impose excessive expense on the family or the community." The bishops' "Ethical and Religious Directives for Catholic Health Care Services" also say, "There should be a presumption in favor of providing nutrition and hydration to all patients, including patients who require medically assisted nutrition and hydration, as long as this is of sufficient benefit to outweigh the burdens involved to the patient."

Such nuances—"sufficient benefit to outweigh the burdens involved"—were largely cast aside [in 2004] by Pope John Paul II when he declared that nutrition and hydration is not treatment, but instead a routine form of care that should be available to everyone, including those in a persistent vegetative state.

"The sick person in a vegetative state, awaiting recovery or a natural end, still has the right to basic health care (nutrition, hydration, cleanliness, warmth, etc.), and to the prevention of complications related to his confinement to bed," John Paul II told a March 2004 conference on Life Sustaining Treatment and Vegetative State: Scientific Advances and Ethical Dilemmas.

"I should like particularly, to underline how the administration of water and food, even when provided by artificial means, always represents a natural means of preserving life, not a medical act," the pope continued. "Its use, furthermore, should be considered, in principle, ordinary and proportionate, and as such morally obligatory, insofar as and until it is seen to have attained its proper finality, which in the present case consists in providing nourishment to the patient and alleviation of his suffering."

Euthanasia by Omission

The pope continued, "Death by starvation or dehydration is, in fact, the only possible outcome as a result of their withdrawal. In this sense, it ends up becoming, if done knowingly and willingly, true and proper euthanasia by omission."

In the year [after] . . . he uttered those words, John Paul II's language had been parsed ("in principle," "insofar as and until") and his intent questioned. Was he speaking authoritatively? But in an area where bishops, theologians and Catholic medical ethicists choose their words with considerable care, the pope's relatively blunt declaration took many, not least administrators at church-run hospitals, by surprise.

The pope's comments have had an effect. Catholic health care agencies worldwide have reviewed their procedures and some ethicists have rethought and rearticulated their positions. But the pontiff's remarks do not amount to a definitive last word on the question of artificially administered food and water.

Disputed Questions

The question of whether artificially provided nutrition and hydration amounts to medical treatment "has remained disputed" with different bishops offering varying views, notes M. Therese Lysaught, associate professor in the Department of Religious Studies at the University of Dayton, Ohio. "Originally these kinds of interventions were meant to assist other forms of medical treatment, as methods to carry a person through a crisis situation" and were "seen as part of an entire medical treatment program," said Lysaught.

In the case of those in a persistent vegetative state, such care, which includes the surgery necessary to place the feeding tube, is "clearly medically administered and is probably rightly categorized as medical treatment," said Lysaught. Which means, she said, "that it then falls under the calculus of 'ordinary' and 'extraordinary' treatment."

Said Connors, "There are intelligent Catholics of goodwill who are on both sides of the fence here. Quite a number of bishops and many, many medical ethicists have taken a different line of thought—that [provision of nutrition and hydration through artificial means] is indeed a medical treatment and subject to the same kind of analysis as any other medical treatment," such as a consideration of the "hoped-for benefits and the burdens that are involved."

Implications for the Schiavo Case

What does that mean for Terri Schiavo?

"I think Terri Schiavo has the fatal pathology of not being able to eat food or drink water which is being bypassed by medically supplied nutrition and hydration," said Connors. "If the nutrition and hydration is ceased, she will die of the underlying pathology, just as when you remove a ventilator the cause of death is the condition that keeps the patient from breathing."

Not so, argues Fr. Michael Orsi, professor of law at Ave Maria University, Naples, Fla.

"Terri Schiavo is not dying of anything—she is just unable to eat ... and we have a moral obligation to hydrate and to give nutrition to someone who is unable to do that for themselves." Said Orsi: "To remove that feeding tube is to kill Terri Schiavo, there is no other intention here."

Orsi draws a distinction between someone suffering a terminal illness and those in a persistent vegetative or minimally conscious state. "If the person is dying and all the nutrition and hydration is doing is prolonging death and interfering with the dying process you might, in fact, have an obligation to stop that. Life is a very sacred thing, but it is not the ultimate." But that is not the case with Schiavo, says Orsi, whose situation is more comparable to that of a baby dependent on adults to provide food and nutrition than to a terminally ill person.

Quality of Life Questions

Underlying the political, social, ethical, legal and religious disputes that surround Schiavo's case is a question: Fifteen years after suffering an incapacitating illness that has left her bedridden and largely unresponsive to the world around her, is Terri Schiavo's life worth living?

It's a question, suggested Orsi, best left unanswered. "How much consciousness is there of someone who has Alzheimer's disease?" he asked. Orsi said he is fearful of the consequences to society if "quality of life" becomes the measure by which such decisions are made.

While allowing that in the case of someone like Schiavo a conscientious Catholic could elect to remove a feeding tube, Lysaught sees considerable merit in doubts raised about the practice. "The church holds that our actions affect not only other people but ourselves and our character, that once I engage in an action where I intend to do something morally evil it becomes easier to do it again," said Lysaught.

Noting that two-dozen national disability rights groups have supported efforts to restore Schiavo's feeding tube, Kilner cautions that "quality of life scales" are a "very dangerous way of approaching the care of people when we don't know what their wishes are."

Connors, meanwhile, argues that society's euthanistic impulse might actually be furthered "if we start mandating certain types of treatment that always must be given in a certain set of circumstances." Part of what is "fueling the movement toward euthanasia and assisted suicide is the very dramatic fear people have that they will end up . . . like Terri Schiavo."

"In hospice care, no one is deprived of the simple amenities of being kept clean and receiving food and water."

Hospice Care Conflicts Sharply with Bioethics

Paul McHugh

In the following excerpt, Paul McHugh contrasts the views of the health-care professionals working in hospices with those of bioethicists. Hospice workers are concerned with providing comfort to those who are terminally ill or severely incapacitated. While they do not use heroic measures to prevent the patient's death, they likewise will not "betray a patient to death." They also help the patient's loved ones to cope with a prolonged period of "life under altered circumstances," which the patient will experience. In contrast to the hands-on experience of hospice workers, bioethicists deal with abstract terms. One of their main functions, according to McHugh, is to rationalize decisions that shorten the lives of severely ill patients. While this view may be looked on with favor by hospital administrators because it reduces the number of costly long-term patients, actual health-care workers strongly oppose such abstract justifications for premature deaths.

Paul McHugh is a neurologist and distinguished service professor at Johns Hopkins University. He is the author of a collection of essays titled The Mind Has Mountains.

Hospice teams are made up of doctors, nurses, social workers, and physiotherapists who together develop a plan to care for someone in an incurable and usually terminal phase

Paul McHugh, "Annihilating Terry Schiavo," *Commentary*, vol. 119, June 2005, pp. 27–32.

of life. In contrast to hospital services, hospice teams do not see time as being "of the essence." Of the essence now is, instead, the development of mutual understanding among all the parties—patient, family, and caregivers—concerning aims and actions suitable to helping the one who suffers. Achieving those goals usually takes time, for everything depends on gaining and retaining the family's confidence that the team really cares about the patient—is committed to doing its best to sustain what can be sustained, to alleviate suffering while at the same time not demanding heroic sacrifices from anyone.

Developing a Plan to Care

This last point is very important. In a hospice, the staff does not provide a ventilator or cardiac monitoring at a patient's bedside—because there is no plan to transfer the patient to an acute treatment center for respiratory or cardiac support. But neither does the staff believe that, for patients with longstanding and incurable conditions, one can or should ignore the possibility of helping them live a less painful life, even if that might mean a less long one. Thus, a hospice will treat the symptoms of certain potentially deadly conditions like bowel obstructions, cardiac arrhythmias, blood clots, and some infections, but will not treat the conditions themselves.

In hospice care, no one is deprived of the simple amenities of being kept clean and receiving food and water. In Terri Schiavo's case, just as the team did not withdraw her bladder catheter, which helped keep her clean, so it did not withdraw the gastric tube, which had similarly been put in place during the rescue phase in order to ease the burden of nursing her. If for some reason the gastric tube had to be removed, the team would surely have tried to sustain nutrition by feeding her with spoon and cup. . . .

Never Betray a Patient to Death

The overarching principle that hospice doctors and nurses strive to represent and exemplify is never to betray a patient to death, or act directly to kill. They may help a patient surrender to death, by forgoing active medical procedures when these provide nothing but empty time and extend the period of suffering. And their particular judgments in this regard may well be challenged as ambiguous—or even arbitrary—by those with a legal mind or an axe to grind. But those judgments are usually clear to everyone working in a hospice, just as the distinction between betrayal and surrender is clear in other situations in life.

It was in this phase of caring for Terri Schiavo that things went badly wrong. As we have seen, her husband had begun to despair for her and for his own future. As far as the public record shows, he seems to have been given little reason to rekindle his hopes. In particular, no functional studies (like an MRI) were done to determine whether her cerebral cortex, the brain region most responsible for coherent behavior, showed any evidence of recovering. Nor did the testimony of bedside observers help. While some thought they saw evidence of slow but tiny steps toward consciousness, others thought that she displayed only reflex reactions.

He was told her diagnosis was "persistent vegetative state." Predictably, this label complicated rather than aided the situation, encouraging those who thought that she no longer existed as an animate being and infuriating those who believed it labeled her a vegetable. That is precisely why most neuropsychiatrists who work in hospices, even though they acknowledge the term's diagnostic accuracy, are reluctant to use it. Instead, they describe patients like Terri Schiavo in the language of neuropathology. Thus, they might have spoken of her as being in a "decorticate" condition [having a badly damaged cerebral cortex], a term that not only indicates the problem but helps everyone—doctors, nurses, family members— think more dispassionately about how to evaluate it.

As these events unfolded, the plan of sustaining her in a hospice fell apart. Her guardian husband could no longer be persuaded to allow her to be fed, and under Florida law he had the right to demand that her nutrition be stopped. The courts were called in, and in the end judges and policemen removed the hospice team from her care, starving her until she died. No one was satisfied with the outcome. It came too slowly to suit her husband, and it came too brutally to comfort her parents. As for the hospice staff, so deeply biased in favor of sustaining life, one can only imagine their anguish. . . .

Unworthy of Life

As soon as Terri Schiavo's case moved into the law courts of Florida, the concept of "life under altered circumstances" went by the boards—and so, necessarily, did any consideration of how to serve such life. Both had been trumped by the concept of "life unworthy of life," and how to end it.

I use the term "life unworthy of life" advisedly. The phrase first appeared a long time ago—as the title of a book published in Germany in 1920, coauthored by a lawyer and a psychiatrist. *Die Freigabe der Vernichtung Lebensunwertes Leben* translates as "Lifting Constraint from the Annihilation of Life Unworthy of Life." Terri Schiavo's husband and his clinical and legal advisers, believing that hers was now a life unworthy of life, sought, and achieved, its annihilation. Claiming to respect her undocumented wish not to live dependently, they were willing to have her suffer pain and, by specific force of law, to block her caregivers from offering her oral feedings of the kind provided to all terminal patients in a hospice—even to the point of prohibiting mouth-soothing ice chips. Everything else flowed from there.

How *could* such a thing happen? This, after all, is not Nazi Germany, where the culture of death foreshadowed in the awful title of that book would reach such horrendous public proportions. But we in this country have our own, home-grown culture of death, whose face is legal and moral and benignly individualistic rather than authoritarian and pseudoscientific. It has many roots, which would require a long historical treatise to unravel, with obligatory chapters considering such factors as the growth of life-sustaining and life-extending technologies and the dilemmas they bring, the increasingly assertive deprecation of medical expertise and understanding in favor of patients' "autonomous" decision-making, the explosion in rights-related personal law and the associated explosion in medical-malpractice suits, and much else besides.

All this has resulted in a steady diminution in the bonds of implicit trust between patients and their doctors and its replacement, in some cases by suspicion or outright hostility, in many other cases by an almost reflexive unwillingness on the part of doctors to impose their own considered, prudential judgments—including their ethical judgments—on the course of treatment. In the meantime, a new discipline has stepped into the breach; its avowed purpose is to help doctors and patients alike reach decisions in difficult situations, and it is now a mandatory subject of study in medical and nursing schools.

Bioethics as Culture of Death

I am speaking of course about bioethics, which came into being roughly contemporaneously with the other developments I have been describing. To the early leaders of this discipline, it was plain that doctors and nurses, hitherto guided by professional codes of conduct and ancient ideals of virtue embedded in the Hippocratic oath or in the career and writings of [famed nurse and activist] Florence Nightingale, were in need of better and more up-to-date instruction. But, being theorists rather than medical practitioners, most bioethicists proved to be uninterested in developing the characters of doctors and nurses. Rather, they were preoccupied with identifying perceived conflicts between the "aims" of doctors and the "rights" of patients, and with prescribing remedies for those conflicts.

Unlike in medicine itself, these remedies are untested and untestable. They have multiplied nevertheless, to the point where they have become fixtures in the lives of all of us, an unquestioned part of our vocabulary, subtly influencing our most basic attitudes toward sickness and health and, above all, our assumptions about how to prepare ourselves for death. The monuments to the bioethicists' principles include Do Not Resuscitate (DNR) orders, the euphemistically named Living Wills, and the legalization of physician-assisted suicide in the state of Oregon. These are not all the same thing, to be sure, and sophisticated arguments can be advanced for each of them; cumulatively, however, they are signposts of our own culture of death.

Hospital administrators are generally pleased with bioethicists and the rationalizations they provide for ceasing care of the helpless and the disabled. By the same token, their presence is generally shunned by doctors and nurses, whose medical and moral vocabulary draws from different sources, and whose training and experience have disposed them in a different direction. To most doctors and nurses, in any case, the idea that one can control the manner and pace of one's dying is largely a fantasy. They have seen what they have seen, and what they know is that at the crucial moments in this process, no document on earth can substitute for the one-on-one judgment, fallible as it may ultimately be, of a sensible, humane, and experienced physician.

Contemporary bioethics has become a natural ally of the culture of death, but the culture of death itself is a perennial human temptation; for onlookers in particular, it offers a reassuring answer ("this is how X would have wanted it") to otherwise excruciating dilemmas, and it can be rationalized every which way till Sunday. In Terri Schiavo's case, it is what won out over the hospice's culture of life, overwhelming by legal means, and by the force of advanced social opinion, the moral and medical command to choose life, to comfort the afflicted, and to teach others how to do the same. The more this culture continues to influence our thinking, the deeper are likely to become the divisions within our society and within our families, the more hardened our hatreds, and the more manifold our fears. More of us will die prematurely; some of us will even be persuaded that we want to.

CHAPTER 4

Upholding Physician-Assisted Suicide in Oregon

Case Overview

Gonzales (formerly Ashcroft) v. Oregon (2006)

In *Gonzales v. Oregon* the U.S. Supreme Court decided the issue of whether the attorney general could use the 1970 Controlled Substances Act (CSA), to prohibit physicians from prescribing drugs explicitly for assisted suicide.

Under the Oregon Death with Dignity Act (ODWDA) it is legal for physicians to prescribe drugs to help terminally ill patients commit suicide. The act, passed by voters in 1994 in a statewide referendum, went into effect in 1997. Upon its taking effect, several members of Congress sent a letter to the attorney general of the United States, Janet Reno, calling for her to use the CSA to forbid physicians from prescribing drugs for assisted suicide. Reno refused, but upon taking office in 2001 the new attorney general, John Ashcroft—who had been one of the congressmen who signed the original letter—issued a directive indicating that physicians who issued patients drugs to commit suicide could be subject to fines or imprisonment.

Recognizing it would make the ODWDA invalid, the state attorney general of Oregon sued to block Ashcroft's directive. The case eventually reached the Supreme Court under the name of *Gonzales v. Oregon* because Alberto Gonzales had now succeeded Ashcroft as U.S. attorney general.

The Court's majority ruled that Ashcroft's directive was unconstitutional. The case was decided on both technical legal issues and broader constitutional ones. On the technical side, the Court determined that the attorney general had no power under the CSA to criminalize certain prescriptions, because the main purpose of the act was to combat recreational drug use. The act was not originally aimed at preventing physician-assisted suicide.

As for constitutional matters, the Court's majority believed that the phrase "legitimate medical purpose" in the Controlled Substances Act could include prescription drugs for suicide. They held that the definition of "legitimate medical purpose" should be determined by the voters of Oregon, just as regulating licensing and conduct of physicians is traditionally left to the states. The majority held that the attorney general's directive was an obvious attempt by the federal government to interfere in an area traditionally reserved to the states.

In his dissent, Justice Antonin Scalia noted that the federal government has long interfered with the states in matters of "public morality." Unless the justices wanted to outlaw all interference in state matters other than those enumerated in the Constitution, claimed Scalia, the Court should be consistent and permit the federal Department of Justice to intervene to stop the Oregon law. He was not convinced that the original intent of the Controlled Substances Act was limited to recreational drugs; the law as written did not define recreational drug use as the only illegitimate purpose. Therefore, under long-standing traditions of deference to federal agencies in defining the meaning of a statute, and in accordance with the opinions of major medical associations and most state legislatures, Scalia felt the attorney general was within his rights to hold that physician-assisted suicide was not a legitimate medical purpose.

> "It is difficult to defend the Attorney
> General's declaration that the [Con-
> trolled Substances Act] impliedly crimi-
> nalizes physician-assisted suicide."

The Court's Decision: Federal Drug Laws Cannot Be Used to Prohibit Physician-Assisted Suicide

Anthony Kennedy

During his service as attorney general of the United States, John Ashcroft issued an instruction stating that the prescription of drugs for physician-assisted suicide, as allowed under the Oregon Death with Dignity Act (ODWDA), violated the federal Controlled Substances Act (CSA) of 1970. The state of Oregon challenged this policy through the courts, as it would effectively mean the end of physician-assisted suicide in Oregon, a policy that had been approved by Oregon voters in a statewide referendum. Oregon's challenge eventually ended up before the Supreme Court, with Ashcroft's successor, Alberto Gonzales, as party to the case.

In the majority opinion, Anthony Kennedy holds that the Controlled Substances Act cannot be used to outlaw the prescription of drugs to be used by the terminally ill to end their lives. While the attorney general argued that these prescriptions did not meet a "legitimate medical purpose," which is one of the requirements for prescribing controlled substances under federal

Anthony Kennedy, majority opinion, *Gonzales v. Oregon*, January 17, 2006.

law, Kennedy and a majority of the justices ruled that this was a matter of debate best left up to the voters of Oregon and the other states.

Anthony Kennedy was appointed to the Supreme Court by President Ronald Reagan in 1988. Considered a moderate, he is often one of the "swing votes" on the Court.

In deciding whether the CSA can be read as prohibiting physician-assisted suicide, we look to the statute's text and design. The statute and our case law amply support the conclusion that Congress regulates medical practice insofar as it bars doctors from using their prescription-writing powers as a means to engage in illicit drug dealing and trafficking as conventionally understood. Beyond this, however, the statute manifests no intent to regulate the practice of medicine generally. The silence is understandable given the structure and limitations of federalism, which allow the States "'great latitude under their police powers to legislate as to the protection of the lives, limbs, health, comfort, and quiet of all persons.'"

States Are Responsible for Regulating Physicians

The structure and operation of the CSA presume and rely upon a functioning medical profession regulated under the States' police powers. The Attorney General can register a physician to dispense controlled substances "if the applicant is authorized to dispense ... controlled substances under the laws of the State in which he practices." When considering whether to revoke a physician's registration, the Attorney General looks not just to violations of federal drug laws; but he "shall" also consider "[t]he recommendation of the appropriate state licensing board or professional disciplinary authority" and the registrant's compliance with state and local drug laws. The very definition of a "practitioner" eligible to prescribe includes physicians "licensed, registered, or otherwise permitted, by the United States or the jurisdiction in which he practices" to dispense controlled substances. Further cautioning against the conclusion that the CSA effectively displaces the States' general regulation of medical practice is the Act's pre-emption provision, which indicates that, absent a positive conflict, none of the Act's provisions should be "construed as indicating an intent on the part of the Congress to occupy the field in which that provision operates . . . to the exclusion of any State law on the same subject matter which would otherwise be within the authority of the State."

Oregon's regime is an example of the state regulation of medical practice that the CSA presupposes. Rather than simply decriminalizing assisted suicide, ODWDA [Oregon Death with Dignity Act] limits its exercise to the attending physicians of terminally ill patients, physicians who must be licensed by Oregon's Board of Medical Examiners. The statute gives attending physicians a central role, requiring them to provide prognoses and prescriptions, give information about palliative alternatives and counseling, and ensure patients are competent and acting voluntarily. Any eligible patient must also get a second opinion from another registered physician, and the statute's safeguards require physicians to keep and submit to inspection detailed records of their actions.

Congress Intended to Fight Recreational Drug Abuse

Even though regulation of health and safety is "primarily, and historically, a matter of local concern," there is no question that the Federal Government can set uniform national standards in these areas. In connection to the CSA, however, we find only one area in which Congress set general, uniform standards of medical practice. Title I of the Comprehensive Drug Abuse Prevention and Control Act of 1970, of which the CSA was Title II, provides that

> [The Secretary (of Health of Human Services)] after consultation with the Attorney General and with national orga-

> nizations representative of persons with knowledge and ex-
> perience in the treatment of narcotic addicts, shall determine
> the appropriate methods of professional practice in the
> medical treatment of the narcotic addiction of various
> classes of narcotic addicts, and shall report thereon from
> time to time to the Congress.

This provision strengthens the understanding of the CSA as a statute combating recreational drug abuse, and also indicates that when Congress wants to regulate medical practice in the given scheme, it does so by explicit language in the statute.

In the face of the CSA's silence on the practice of medicine generally and its recognition of state regulation of the medical profession it is difficult to defend the Attorney General's declaration that the statute impliedly criminalizes physician-assisted suicide. This difficulty is compounded by the CSA's consistent delegation of medical judgments to the Secretary and its otherwise careful allocation of powers for enforcing the limited objects of the CSA. The Government's attempt to meet this challenge rests, for the most part, on the CSA's requirement that every Schedule II drug be dispensed pursuant to a "written prescription of a practitioner." A prescription, the Government argues, necessarily implies that the substance is being made available to a patient for a legitimate medical purpose. The statute, in this view, requires an anterior judgment about the term "medical" or "medicine." The Government contends ordinary usage of these words ineluctably [necessarily] refers to a healing or curative art, which by these terms cannot embrace the intentional hastening of a patient's death. It also points to the teachings of Hippocrates, the positions of prominent medical organizations, the Federal Government, and the judgment of the 49 States that have not legalized physician-assisted suicide as further support for the proposition that the practice is not legitimate medicine.

No Broad Federal Authority to Regulate Medicine

On its own, this understanding of medicine's boundaries is at least reasonable. The primary problem with the Government's argument, however, is its assumption that the CSA impliedly authorizes an Executive officer to bar a use simply because it may be inconsistent with one reasonable understanding of medical practice. Viewed alone, the prescription requirement may support such an understanding, but statutes "should not be read as a series of unrelated and isolated provisions." The CSA's substantive provisions and their arrangement undermine this assertion of an expansive federal authority to regulate medicine.

The statutory criteria for deciding what substances are controlled, determinations which are central to the Act, consistently connect the undefined term "drug abuse" with addiction or abnormal effects on the nervous system. When the Attorney General schedules drugs, he must consider a substance's psychic or physiological dependence liability. To classify a substance in Schedules II through V, the Attorney General must find abuse of the drug leads to psychological or physical dependence. Indeed, the differentiation of Schedules II through V turns in large part on a substance's habit-forming potential: The more addictive a substance, the stricter the controls. When Congress wanted to extend the CSA's regulation to substances not obviously habit forming or psychotropic, moreover, it relied not on Executive ingenuity, but rather on specific legislation.

The statutory scheme with which the CSA is intertwined further confirms a more limited understanding of the prescription requirement. When the Secretary [of Health and Human Services] considers FDA [Food and Drug Administration] approval of a substance with "stimulant, depressant, or hallucinogenic effect," he must forward the information to the Attorney General for possible scheduling. Shedding light on

Congress' understanding of drug abuse, this requirement appears under the heading "Abuse potential." Similarly, when Congress prepared to implement the Convention on Psychotropic Substances, it did so through the CSA.

The Interpretive Rule rests on a reading of the prescription requirement that is persuasive only to the extent one scrutinizes the provision without the illumination of the rest of the statute. Viewed in its context, the prescription requirement is better understood as a provision that ensures patients use controlled substances under the supervision of a doctor so as to prevent addiction and recreational abuse. As a corollary, the provision also bars doctors from peddling to patients who crave the drugs for those prohibited uses. To read prescriptions for assisted suicide as constituting "drug abuse" under the CSA is discordant with the phrase's consistent use throughout the statute, not to mention its ordinary meaning.

No Federal Ban on Prescriptions Used for Suicide

The Government's interpretation of the prescription requirement also fails under the objection that the Attorney General is an unlikely recipient of such broad authority, given the Secretary's primacy in shaping medical policy under the CSA, and the statute's otherwise careful allocation of decision-making powers. Just as the conventions of expression indicate that Congress is unlikely to alter a statute's obvious scope and division of authority through muffled hints, the background principles of our federal system also belie the notion that Congress would use such an obscure grant of authority to regulate areas traditionally supervised by the States' police power. It is unnecessary even to consider the application of clear statement requirements, or presumptions against pre-emption . . . to reach this commonsense conclusion. For all these reasons, we conclude the CSA's prescription requirement does not authorize the Attorney General to bar dispensing controlled substances for assisted suicide in the face of a state medical regime permitting such conduct.

The Government, in the end, maintains that the prescription requirement delegates to a single Executive officer the power to effect a radical shift of authority from the States to the Federal Government to define general standards of medical practice in every locality. The text and structure of the CSA show that Congress did not have this far-reaching intent to alter the federal-state balance and the congressional role in maintaining it.

> "If the term 'legitimate *medical purpose'*
> has any meaning, it surely excludes the
> prescription of drugs to produce death."

Dissenting Opinion: The Federal Government Can Ban the Prescribing of Drugs for Suicide

Antonin Scalia

In 2001 attorney general John Ashcroft issued a rule interpreting the Controlled Substances Act (CSA) of 1970 that concluded that doctors could be punished for prescribing drugs for assisted suicide. This ruling clashed with the Oregon Death with Dignity Act (ODWDA) that allowed doctors to give patients drugs with which to end their lives. Oregon fought the issue in the legal system and the case ended up before the Supreme Court.

In the following excerpt from his dissenting opinion, Antonin Scalia makes the case that physician-assisted suicide is not a "legitimate medical purpose" as required for a legal prescription under the CSA. He notes that medical organizations as well as state legislatures (with the exception of Oregon) are unanimous in agreeing that suicide is not a "legitimate medical purpose." Rather than looking at the current state of medical ethics, according to Scalia, the majority of the Court has injected their personal views of what "legitimate medical purpose" should mean. Scalia is not convinced by the Court's claim that the regulation of doctors should be left to the states; he notes that the United States Congress has preempted state functions, with Court approval, for many decades.

Antonin Scalia, dissenting opinion, *Gonzales v. Oregon*, January 17, 2006.

Antonin Scalia was appointed to the Supreme Court by President Ronald Reagan in 1986. He is known as a conservative stalwart on the Court, devoted to a strict interpretation of the Constitution.

Even if the Directive [the interpretive rule issued by the attorney general] were entitled to no deference whatever, the most reasonable interpretation of the Regulation and of the statute would produce the same result. Virtually every relevant source of authoritative meaning confirms that the phrase "legitimate medical purpose" does not include intentionally assisting suicide. "Medicine" refers to "[t]he science and art dealing with the prevention, cure, or alleviation of disease." The use of the word "legitimate" connotes an *objective* standard of "medicine," and our presumption that the CSA creates a uniform federal law regulating the dispensation of controlled substances, means that this objective standard must be a federal one. As recounted in detail in the memorandum for the Attorney General that is attached as an appendix to the Directive (OLC [Office of Legal Counsel] Memo), virtually every medical authority from Hippocrates[1] to the current American Medical Association (AMA) confirms that assisting suicide has seldom or never been viewed as a form of "prevention, cure, or alleviation of disease," and (even more so) that assisting suicide is not a "legitimate" branch of that "science and art." Indeed, the AMA has determined that "'[p]hysician-assisted suicide is fundamentally incompatible with the physician's role as a healer.'" [According to the OLC memo,] "[T]he overwhelming weight of authority in judicial decisions, the past and present policies of nearly all of the States and of the Federal Government, and the clear, firm and unequivocal views of the leading associations within the American medical and nursing professions, establish that assisting in suicide . . . is not a legitimate medical purpose."

---

1. Hippocrates was an ancient Greek physician. He created an oath that spelled out the ethics of the medical profession and that is taken by doctors to this day.

Court Confused on Current Medical Ethics

In the face of this "overwhelming weight of authority," the Court's admission that "[o]n its own, this understanding of medicine's boundaries is *at least reasonable*," tests the limits of understatement. The only explanation for such a distortion is that the Court confuses the *normative* inquiry of what the boundaries of medicine *should be*—which it is laudably hesitant to undertake—with the *objective* inquiry of what the accepted definition of "medicine" *is*. The same confusion is reflected in the Court's remarkable statement that "[t]he primary problem with the Government's argument . . . is its assumption that the CSA impliedly authorizes an Executive officer to bar a use simply because it may be inconsistent with *one reasonable understanding* of medical practice." The fact that many in Oregon believe that the boundaries of "legitimate medicine" *should be* extended to include assisted suicide does not change the fact that the overwhelming weight of authority (including the 47 States that condemn physician-assisted suicide) confirms that they have not yet been so extended. . . .

The Court contends that the phrase "legitimate medical purpose" *cannot* be read to establish a broad, uniform federal standard for the medically proper use of controlled substances. But it also rejects the most plausible alternative proposition, urged by the State, that any use authorized under state law constitutes a "legitimate medical purpose." (The Court is perhaps leery of embracing this position because the State candidly admitted at oral argument that, on its view, a State could exempt from the CSA's coverage the use of morphine to achieve euphoria.) Instead, the Court reverse-engineers an approach somewhere between a uniform national standard and a state-by-state approach, holding (with no basis in the CSA's text) that "legitimate medical purpose" refers to *all* uses of drugs unrelated to "addiction and recreational abuse." Thus, though the Court pays lip service to state autonomy, its standard for "legitimate medical purpose" is in fact a hazily defined *federal* standard based on its purposive reading of the CSA, and extracted from obliquely relevant sections of the Act. In particular, relying on its observation that the criteria for scheduling controlled substances are primarily concerned with "addiction or abnormal effects on the nervous systems," the Court concludes that the CSA's prescription requirement must be interpreted in light of this narrow view of the statute's purpose.

A Broad Mandate

Even assuming, however, that the *principal* concern of the CSA is the curtailment of "addiction and recreational abuse," there is no reason to think that this is its *exclusive* concern. We have repeatedly observed that Congress often passes statutes that sweep more broadly than the main problem they were designed to address [The Court has written:] "[S]tatutory prohibitions often go beyond the principal evil to cover reasonably comparable evils, and it is ultimately the provisions of our laws rather than the principal concerns of our legislators by which we are governed."

The scheduling provisions of the CSA on which the Court relies confirm that the CSA's "design" is not as narrow as the Court asserts. In making scheduling determinations, the Attorney General must not only consider a drug's "psychic or physiological dependence liability" as the Court points out, but must also consider such broad factors as "[t]he state of current scientific knowledge regarding the drug or other substance," and (most notably) "[w]hat, if any, risk there is to the public health." If the latter factor were limited to addiction-related health risks, as the Court supposes, it would be redundant of [section] 811(c)(7) [of the CSA]. Moreover, in making registration determinations regarding manufacturers and distributors, the Attorney General "shall" consider "such *other* factors as may be relevant to and consistent with the public health and safety,"—over and above the risk of "diversion" of controlled substances. And, most relevant of all, in registering and deregistering *physicians*, the Attorney General "may deny an application for such registration if he determines that the issuance of such registration would be inconsistent with the public interest," and in making that determination "shall" consider "[s]uch other conduct which may threaten the public health and safety." *All* of these provisions, not just those selectively cited by the Court, shed light upon the CSA's repeated references to the undefined term "abuse."

By disregarding all these public-interest, public-health, and public-safety objectives, and limiting the CSA to "addiction and recreational abuse," the Court rules out the prohibition of anabolic-steroid use for bodybuilding purposes. It seeks to avoid this consequence by invoking the Anabolic Steroids Control Act of 1990. But the only effect of that legislation is to make anabolic steroids controlled drugs under Schedule III of the CSA. If the only *basis* for control is (as the Court says) "addiction and recreational abuse," dispensation of these drugs for bodybuilding could not be proscribed.

No Elephant in a Mousehole

With regard to the CSA's registration provisions, the Court argues that the statute cannot fairly be read to "'hide elephants in mouseholes'" by delegating to the Attorney General the power to determine the legitimacy of medical practices in "'vague terms or ancillary provisions.'" This case bears not the remotest resemblance to *Whitman* [*v. American Trucking Assns. Inc.* (2001)], which held that "Congress . . . does not alter *the fundamental details* of a regulatory scheme in vague terms or ancillary provisions" (emphasis added). The Attorney General's power to issue regulations against questionable uses of controlled substances in no way alters "the fundamental details" of the CSA. I am aware of only four areas in which the Department of Justice has exercised that power to regulate uses of controlled substances *unrelated* to "addiction and recreational abuse" as the Court apparently understands that phrase: assisted suicide, aggressive pain management therapy, anabolic-steroid use, and cosmetic weight-loss therapy. There is no indication that enforcement in these areas interferes with the prosecution of "drug abuse" as the Court understands it. Unlike in *Whitman*, the Attorney General's *additional* power to address other forms of drug "abuse" does *absolutely nothing* to undermine the central features of this regulatory scheme. . . .

Finally, respondents [the state of Oregon] argue that the Attorney General must defer to state-law judgments about what constitutes legitimate medicine, on the grounds that Congress must speak clearly to impose such a uniform federal standard upon the States. But no line of our clear-statement cases is applicable here. The canon of avoidance does not apply, since the Directive does not push the outer limits of Congress's commerce power, or impinge on a core aspect of state sovereignty. The clear-statement rule based on the presumption against pre-emption does not apply because the Directive does not pre-empt any state law. And finally, no clear statement is required on the ground that the Directive intrudes upon an area traditionally reserved exclusively to the States, because the Federal Government has pervasively regulated the dispensation of drugs for over 100 years. It would be a novel and massive expansion of the clear-statement rule to apply it in a commerce case *not involving pre-emption or constitutional avoidance*, merely because Congress has chosen to prohibit conduct that a State has made a contrary policy judgment to permit.

In sum, the Directive's first conclusion—namely that physician-assisted suicide is not a "legitimate medical purpose"—is supported both by the deference we owe to the agency's interpretation of its own regulations and by the deference we owe to its interpretation of the statute. The other two conclusions—(2) that prescribing controlled drugs to assist suicide violates the CSA, and (3) that such conduct is also "inconsistent with the public interest"—are inevitable consequences of that first conclusion. Moreover, the third conclusion, standing alone, is one that the Attorney General is authorized to make.

The Court's decision today is perhaps driven by a feeling that the subject of assisted suicide is none of the Federal Government's business. It is easy to sympathize with that position. The prohibition or deterrence of assisted suicide is certainly not among the enumerated powers conferred on the United States by the Constitution, and it is within the realm of public morality (*bonos mores*) traditionally addressed by the so-called police power of the States. But then, neither is prohibiting the recreational use of drugs or discouraging drug addiction among the enumerated powers. From an early time in our national history, the Federal Government has used its enumerated powers, such as its power to regulate interstate commerce, for the purpose of protecting public morality—for example, by banning the interstate shipment of lottery tickets, or the interstate transport of women for immoral purposes. Unless we are to repudiate a long and well-established principle of our jurisprudence, using the federal commerce power to prevent assisted suicide is unquestionably permissible. The question before us is not whether Congress *can* do this, or even whether Congress *should* do this; but simply whether Congress *has* done this in the CSA. I think there is no doubt that it has. If the term "*legitimate* medical purpose" has any meaning, it surely excludes the prescription of drugs to produce death.

> *"Physician-assisted suicide has never been, and is not now, a generally recognized and accepted medical practice in the United States."*

Prescribing Drugs for Assisted Suicide Does Not Serve a Legitimate Medical Purpose

Sheldon Bradshaw and Robert J. Delahunty

In this excerpt from a Department of Justice memorandum, Sheldon Bradshaw and Robert Delahunty argue that the dispensing of drugs for assisted suicide violates federal drug regulations. Under federal law, physicians are authorized to dispense drugs for a "legitimate medical purpose." The authors argue that assisted suicide does not meet this criterion. First, they contend, the vast majority of state governments, as well as the federal government do not agree that assisted suicide is a proper medical procedure. Second, major professional medical organizations agree that assisted suicide does not qualify as a medical treatment. Because assisted suicide is not legitimate medical treatment the federal government can forbid Oregon physicians from prescribing or administering the drugs necessary for patients to kill themselves, despite the state's legalization of this practice, Bradshaw and Delahunty maintain.

When this memo was written, Sheldon Bradshaw was deputy assistant attorney general, and Robert J. Delahunty served as special counsel for the Justice Department. Bradshaw is currently

Sheldon Bradshaw and Robert J. Delahunty, "Whether Physician-Assisted Suicide Serves a 'Legitimate Medical Purpose' Under the Drug Enforcement Administration's Regulations Implementing the Controlled Substances Act," *Issues in Law & Medicine*, vol. 17, 2002, pp. 269–282. Reproduced by permission.

chief counsel for the Food and Drug Administration, and Delahunty is currently a law professor at the University of Saint Thomas in Saint Paul, Minnesota.

You [attorney general John Ashcroft] have asked for our opinion whether a physician who assists in a patient's suicide by prescribing a controlled substance has a "legitimate medical purpose" within the meaning of a regulation of the Drug Enforcement Administration (DEA), 21 C.F.R. [Section] 1306.04(a) (2000), if the physician is immune from liability under a state law such as the Oregon "Death with Dignity Act" for assisting in a suicide in such a manner. In our view, assisting in suicide, even in a manner permitted by state law, is not a "legitimate medical purpose" under the DEA regulation, and, accordingly, dispensing controlled substances for this purpose violates the Controlled Substances Act, which the DEA regulation implements. . . .

We understand that physician-assisted suicide typically involves the use of a lethal dose of a combination of drugs, including controlled substances. First, the patient is sedated using either a barbiturate (e.g., sodium pentothal), or an opiate (e.g., morphine). Then, one or more drugs are used to paralyze the muscles and/or to stop the heart. The sedatives involved in these procedures are controlled substances under the CSA. Most lawfully available opiates and barbiturates are in Schedule II of the CSA, the most strictly regulated category of substances available for non-research purposes.

In our opinion, assisting in suicide is not a "legitimate medical purpose" within the meaning of [DEA regulations] that would justify a physician's dispensing controlled substances. That interpretation, which the DEA itself originally adopted before being overruled by Attorney General [Janet] Reno, is the best reading of the regulatory language: it is firmly supported by the case law, by the traditional and current policies and practices of the Federal government and of the overwhelming majority of the States, and by the dominant views of the American medical and nursing professions.

Court Cases

The case law demonstrates that the CSA forbids dispensing controlled substances except in the course of accepted medical practice, and that physician-assisted suicide is outside the boundaries of such practice.

In [*United States v.*] *Moore* (1975), the Supreme Court in effect approved a jury instruction under which a physician would be held criminally liable for dispensing controlled substances in violation of [Controlled Substances Act, Section 841, "unlawful acts"] unless the physician was acting "in the usual course of professional practice and in accordance with a standard of medical practice generally recognized and accepted in the United States." The lower courts have followed *Moore* in requiring that a physician's actions conform to standards "generally recognized and accepted" throughout the nation. For example, in *United States v. Vamos* (1986) the court stated that:

> To permit a practitioner to substitute his or her views of what is good medical practice for standards generally recognized and accepted in the United States would be to weaken the enforcement of our drug laws in a critical area. As the Supreme Court noted in *Moore*, 'Congress intended the CSA to strengthen rather than weaken the prior drug laws.'

As the courts have found, physician-assisted suicide has never been, and is not now, a generally recognized and accepted medical practice in the United States. On the contrary, the American legal system and the American medical profession alike have consistently condemned the practice in the past and continue to do so.

In *Washington v. Glucksberg* (1997) the Supreme Court upheld a state prohibition against causing or aiding a suicide against a challenge that, as applied to physicians assisting terminally ill, mentally competent patients, the prohibition offended the requirements of substantive due process. The Court began its analysis by examining "our Nation's history, legal traditions, and practices." The Court found that "[i]n almost every State—indeed, in almost every western democracy—it is a crime to assist a suicide. The States' assisted-suicide bans are not innovations. Rather, they are longstanding expressions of the States' commitment to the protection and preservation of all human life.". . .

Further, the Court discussed the "serious, thoughtful examinations of physician-assisted suicide and other similar issues" now going on in the States. It referred in particular to the work of New York State's Task Force on Life and the Law, a commission composed of doctors, ethicists, lawyers, religious leaders and interested laymen charged with recommending public policy on issues raised by medical advances. The Court noted that after studying physician-assisted suicide, the Task Force had unanimously concluded that "[l]egalizing assisted suicide and euthanasia would pose profound risks to many individuals who are ill and vulnerable. . . . [T]he potential dangers of this dramatic change in public policy would outweigh any benefit that might be achieved."

Summarizing its review of the American legal tradition's view of assisted suicide, the Court said:

> Attitudes toward suicide itself have changed . . . , but our laws have consistently condemned, and continue to prohibit, assisting suicide. Despite changes in medical technology and notwithstanding an increased emphasis on the importance of end-of-life decision making, we have not retreated from this prohibition.

State and Federal Policy

As detailed in *Washington v. Glucksberg*, state law and policy, with the sole exception of Oregon's, emphatically oppose assisted suicide. Assisted suicide has long been prohibited at common law, and at least forty States and territories have laws explicitly prohibiting the practice. "In the two hundred and five years of our [national] existence no constitutional right to aid in killing oneself has ever been asserted and upheld by a court of final jurisdiction." The only state supreme court to decide the matter has rejected recognition of an enforceable right to assisted suicide under that State's constitution.

State statutes banning assisted suicide trace back a century or more in many cases. They have not been kept on the books through oversight or neglect. . . .

Federal policy fully accords with the views that prevail in every State except Oregon. As noted in *Glucksberg*, the Assisted Suicide Funding Restriction Act of 1997, was signed into law on April 30, 1997. The Act was approved in the House of Representatives by a 398-to-16 vote and in the Senate by a 99-to-0 vote. The Act bans Federal funding of assisted suicide, euthanasia, or mercy killing through Medicaid, Medicare, military and Federal employee health plans, the veterans' health care system, or other Federally funded programs. In the "Findings" preceding the Act's substantive restrictions, Congress stated that "[a]ssisted suicide, euthanasia, and mercy killing have been criminal offenses throughout the United States and, under current law, it would be unlawful to provide services in support of such illegal activities." Then, after taking note that the Oregon "Death With Dignity Act" might soon become operative, Congress determined that it would "not provid[e] Federal financial assistance in support of assisted suicide, euthanasia, and mercy killing and intends that Federal funds not be used to promote such activities." In general, Congress stated that its purpose was "to continue current Federal policy by providing explicitly that Federal funds may not be used to pay for items and services (including assistance) the purpose of which is to cause (or assist in causing) the suicide, euthanasia, or mercy killing of any individual."

Even before the enactment of the Assisted Suicide Funding Restriction Act of 1997, it was the policy of the Federal Government not to recognize physician-assisted suicide as a legitimate medical practice. As Acting Solicitor General Walter Dellinger noted in 1996 in the United States Brief in *Glucksberg*:

> The United States owns and operates numerous health care facilities which ... do not permit physicians to assist patients in committing suicide by providing lethal dosages of medication. The Department of Veterans Affairs (VA), which operates 173 medical centers, 126 nursing homes, and 55 inpatient hospices, has a policy manual that ... forbids 'the active hastening of the moment of death.' ... The military services, which operate 124 centers, the Indian Health service, which operates 43 hospitals, and the National Institutes of Health, which operate a clinical center, follow a similar practice.... No federal law ... either authorizes or accommodates physician assisted suicide.

Other Federal agencies have taken similar views in the past. The Hyde Letter noted that "[t]he Health Care Financing Administration has stated that physician-assisted suicide is not 'reasonable and necessary' to the diagnosis and treatment of disease or injury and is therefore barred from reimbursement under Medicare."[1] [DEA] Administrator [Thomas] Constantine's reply stated that a review of "a number of cases, briefs, law review articles and state laws relating to physician-assisted suicide" and "a thorough review of prior administrative cases in which physicians have dispensed controlled substances for other than a 'legitimate medical purpose'" demonstrated "that delivering, dispensing or prescribing a controlled substance with the intent of assisting a suicide would not be under any current definition a 'legitimate medical purpose.'"

---

1. In 1997 Congressman Henry Hyde of Illinois wrote the director of the Drug Enforcement Administration asking for a determination of whether prescribing drugs for assisted suicide served a "legitimate medical purpose."

Finally, Federal medical policy *since* the enactment of the Assisted Suicide Funding Restriction Act also supports the conclusion that physician-assisted suicide is not a legitimate medical practice. In 1999, the Surgeon General sought to classify suicide as a serious public health problem and to intensify suicide prevention efforts, especially among high risk groups such as the sick and elderly, who often suffer from undiagnosed depression and inadequately treated pain. Dispensing controlled substances to assist the suicides of some of the most vulnerable members of American society is manifestly inconsistent with the Surgeon General's policy.

Views of the Medical and Nursing Professions

The leading organizations of the American medical profession have repeatedly, and recently, expressed the profession's condemnation of physician-assisted suicide. The American Medical Association (AMA), joined by the American Nurses Association (ANA), the American Psychiatric Association, and 43 other national medical organizations, filed a brief in the *Glucksberg* case declaring that "[t]he ethical prohibition against physician-assisted suicide is a cornerstone of medical ethics" and that physician-assisted suicide is "'fundamentally incompatible with the physician's role as healer.'" More specifically, the AMA's Brief said:

> The power to assist in intentionally taking the life of a patient is antithetical to the central mission of healing that guides both medicine and nursing. It is a power that most physicians and nurses do not want and could not control. Once established, the right to physician-assisted suicide would create profound danger for many ill persons with undiagnosed depression and inadequately treated pain, for whom physician-assisted suicide rather than good palliative care could become the norm. At greatest risk would be those with the least access to palliative care—the poor, the elderly, and members of minority groups....

As the Court noted in *Glucksberg*, the AMA's Code of Ethics condemns physician-assisted suicide as fundamentally incompatible with the physician's role as a healer. Largely on the basis of the AMA's position, the Court found that the State of Washington had "an interest in protecting the integrity and ethics of the medical profession" when it prohibited physician-assisted suicide.

The AMA took the same unequivocal position in hearings before Congress on the subject of assisted suicide. Dr. [Lannie R.] Bristow [then president of the AMA] testified:

> The AMA believes that physician-assisted suicide is unethical and fundamentally inconsistent with the pledge physicians make to devote themselves to healing and to life. . . . AMA takes seriously its role as a leader in issues of medical and professional ethics. The AMA's code of ethics serves as the profession's defining document as to what is right versus what is wrong in medical practice, and such issues are critical to our professionalism and our role as healers. My primary obligation as a physician is to first be an advocate for my patient. If my patient is understandably apprehensive or afraid of his or her own mortality, I need to provide information, support, and comfort, not help them avoid the issues of death.

The ANA, a national organization representing 2.2 million registered nurses, submitted written testimony to Congress at the same hearing. Included in the ANA's submission was the organization's *Position Statement on Assisted Suicide* (1994). The *Position Statement* succinctly summarizes the ANA's view of nurse-assisted suicide as follows:

> The American Nurses Association believes that the nurse should not participate in assisted suicide. Such an act is in violation of the *Code for Nurses with Interpretive Statements* and the ethical traditions of the profession.

Scholars have observed that the norms of the medical and nursing professions with respect to physician-assisted suicide, which reflect the experience and the reflection of centuries, are more compelling now than ever.

To be sure, it has been claimed that physician-assisted suicide has become a common, if also usually clandestine, practice. But the claim is questionable. The American Geriatrics Society, for example, has stated that the Society's leadership "is unfamiliar with situations in which this is true, and it seems unlikely. Three-quarters of all deaths happen in institutions where a regularized endeavor would require the collusion of a large number of persons, which seems implausible. Little reliable evidence characterizes the rate and nature of actual instances of [physician-assisted suicide]." Moreover, even if there were reliable evidence that unacknowledged physician-assisted suicide was not infrequent, that fact would hardly invalidate the *normative* judgments of the AMA and other medical groups that emphatically condemn the practice. By parity of reasoning, if it could be shown that physicians violated traditional medical canons of ethics more often than is usually supposed, e.g., by engaging in sexual relations with their patients or disclosing patient confidences, it would follow that the evidence of such deviations overturned the professional standards prohibiting such misconduct.

Overwhelming Evidence Against Assisted Suicide

Thus, the overwhelming weight of authority in judicial decisions, the past and present policies of nearly all of the States and of the Federal Government, and the clear, firm and unequivocal views of the leading associations within the American medical and nursing professions, establish that assisting in suicide is not an activity undertaken in the course of professional medical practice and is not a legitimate medical purpose. Indeed, we think it fair to say that physician-assisted suicide should not be considered a *medical* procedure at all. Here we follow an *amicus* brief filed in *Glucksberg* by a group of fifty bioethics professors, who declared that physician-assisted suicide "is not a medical procedure, and medicalizing an act runs the risk of making an otherwise unacceptable act appear acceptable." As this brief points out, assisted suicide does not require any medical knowledge whatever, nor does it necessarily depend on access to any prescribed drugs or to medical services. Indeed, the country's most prominent partisan of assisted suicide, Jack Kevorkian, has often used the entirely nonmedical method of carbon monoxide poisoning. It is plainly a fallacy to assume that a procedure must be "medical" because it is performed by a physician rather than, say, by a family member, or because it involves the use of a drug that a physician has prescribed.

Accordingly, we conclude that assisting in suicide is not a "legitimate medical purpose" that would justify a physician's dispensing controlled substances consistent with the CSA.

> *"The Oregon Death With Dignity Act has provided choices to terminally ill Oregonians and has made Oregon a national leader in end-of-life care."*

The Supreme Court Rightly Rejects Federal Efforts to Stop Physician-Assisted Suicide

Valerie Vollmar

This excerpt is an analysis of the Supreme Court's reasoning in upholding Oregon's Death with Dignity Act. Law professor Valerie Vollmar points out that the Court was unusually critical of the federal government's trying to interfere with the state law in this area. The majority notes that the case was brought by John Ashcroft, who as a senator had supported attempts to overturn Oregon's law. The implication is that Ashcroft in his position as attorney general is merely pursuing his personal preferences, rather than the law. Vollmar also notes that Gonzales v. Oregon involved the balance of power between states and the federal government. Various state legislatures were debating the merits of physician-assisted suicide, and the Ashcroft decision was an attempt to cut short this process. Vollmar also summarizes Justice Antonin Scalia's dissent; however, her conclusion leaves no doubt that she supports the Oregon law. The decision in Gonzales v. Oregon *leads her to believe that Congress will have difficulty in trying to overturn the Oregon voters' decision to legalize physician-assisted suicide via federal legislation.*

Valerie Vollmar, "The Supreme Court and Death with Dignity in Oregon," *Jurist*, February 1, 2006. Copyright © Bernard J. Hibbitts, 2006. Reproduced by permission of the author.

Valerie Vollmar is a professor at Willamette University College of Law in Salem, Oregon. She is an expert in the legal aspects of physician-assisted suicide.

Although Oregon voters passed the Oregon Death With Dignity Act (ODWDA) [in 1994], the opponents of physician-assisted suicide have been relentless in their efforts to overturn Oregon's law. A constitutional challenge in the federal courts delayed implementation of the ODWDA for three years. Just before the federal litigation ended, voters rejected a referendum measure from the Oregon legislature that would have repealed the new law.

Soon after, at the request of Congressional leaders, the director of the Drug Enforcement Administration [DEA] ruled that physician-assisted suicide was not a "legitimate medical purpose" under the federal Controlled Substances Act (CSA). Thus, Oregon doctors and pharmacists who participated in physician-assisted suicide were at risk of losing their licenses to prescribe and dispense essential drugs such as morphine and barbiturates. Six months later, however, Attorney General Janet Reno reversed the DEA director's ruling.

Longtime Opposition to Assisted Suicide

Congress tried unsuccessfully in 1998 and 1999 to overturn the ODWDA by passing federal legislation. Senator John Ashcroft supported both bills. Within months after President [George W.] Bush took office, Attorney General Ashcroft issued an interpretive rule (the Ashcroft Directive) declaring that physician-assisted suicide is not a "legitimate medical purpose" under the CSA. The Oregon Attorney General sued, and the court permitted a physician, a pharmacist, and several terminally ill patients to intervene.

The U.S. District Court (2002) and the Ninth Circuit Court of Appeals (2004) enjoined [prohibited] enforcement of the Ashcroft Directive. Both courts decided the case based on the CSA, finding it unnecessary to reach the parties' administrative and constitutional law arguments.

On January 17 of [2006] the US Supreme Court affirmed the lower courts. Justice [Anthony] Kennedy, who wrote the majority opinion, was joined by Justices [John Paul] Stevens, [Sandra Day] O'Connor, [David] Souter, [Ruth Bader] Ginsburg, and [Stephen] Breyer. Justice [Antonin] Scalia was joined in his dissenting opinion by Chief Justice [John] Roberts and Justice [Clarence] Thomas. Justice Thomas also wrote a separate dissenting opinion, arguing that the Court's decision was inconsistent with its recent opinion in the California medical marijuana case.

The majority and dissenting justices agreed that the question was whether the CSA allowed the Attorney General to prohibit doctors from prescribing regulated drugs for use in physician-assisted suicide, notwithstanding a state law permitting the practice. The two sides disagreed about everything else.

The opinions consist in large measure of a rather dry, technical discussion of the various levels of deference . . . that might be accorded to the Attorney General as an executive officer. The majority concluded that Ashcroft was not entitled to any level of deference in his decision to issue the Ashcroft Directive; moreover, the CSA did not give Ashcroft authority to regulate the practice of medicine generally. In contrast, the dissent concluded that the Ashcroft Directive was valid . . . , was supported by the language of the CSA itself, and reflected the "overwhelming weight of authority" that physician-assisted suicide is not within the boundaries of medical practice.

The analysis of [the legal] issues in the majority and dissenting opinions is likely to be of great interest to administrative law scholars. The rest of us, though, may find other aspects of the opinions much more fascinating.

Sharp Criticism of Government Case

The majority opinion does not simply say that Ashcroft was misguided in interpreting the extent of his authority. Rather, the justices seem quite critical of Ashcroft's actions.

For example, the majority opinion quotes the statement in *Washington v. Glucksberg* [1997] that "Americans are engaged in an earnest and profound debate about the morality, legality, and practicality of physician-assisted suicide," a debate that Ashcroft obviously tried to terminate. The opinion also notes that Ashcroft supported efforts to curtail assisted suicide while he was a Senator and that he did not consult with Oregon or anyone outside the Justice Department before issuing the Directive, even though he had promised Oregon's Attorney General an opportunity to participate in any discussion of the issue. The opinion further points out that the CSA places the responsibility for making medical judgments on the Secretary of Health and Human Services and not on the Attorney General, who "lacks medical expertise." Indeed, the opinion suggests that the Attorney General's understanding of whether physician-assisted suicide constitutes proper medical practice is not the only reasonable understanding of medical practice.

Other observations in the majority opinion are even more pointed. The justices say that the Attorney General "claims extraordinary authority" that would in effect allow him to criminalize even the actions of registered physicians, whenever they "engage in conduct he deems illegitimate." Moreover, according to the majority, Congress does not implicitly delegate such broad and unusual authority (Congress "does not, one might say, hide elephants in mouseholes").

Finally, the majority opinion cites the principles of federalism, which give the states great latitude under their police powers to regulate matters such as the practice of medicine. The concluding language of the opinion is especially interesting in light of the current struggle over the extent of executive powers: The Government, in the end, maintains that the [CSA] delegates to a single Executive officer the power to effect a radical shift of authority from the States to the Federal Government to define general standards of medical practice in every locality. The text and structure of the CSA show that Congress did not have this far-reaching intent to alter the federal-state balance and the congressional role in maintaining it.

A Naked Value Judgment

As always, the dissenting opinion shows Justice Scalia's gift for using engaging language in support of a detailed legal analysis. He criticizes the majority justices for their "unremitting failure to distinguish among [the] different propositions in the Directive," their creation of a new "parroting regulation" . . . , and their "demonstrably false," "irrelevant," and "manifestly erroneous" conclusions.

On the broader question of physician-assisted suicide itself, Justice Scalia is scathing in his criticism of the majority's view that physician-assisted suicide could be a reasonable understanding of medicine's boundaries, arguing that virtually every relevant authoritative source confirms that intentionally assisting suicide is not a "legitimate medical purpose." He acknowledges that the legitimacy of physician-assisted suicide ultimately rests on "a naked value judgment" but concludes that the federal government may use its powers for the purpose of "protecting public morality." The fact that Chief Justice Roberts joined in his first dissenting opinion in this case may be especially significant given the dissent's views on federalism and public morality.

Oregon Law Safe and Effective

For more than eight years, the Oregon Death With Dignity Act has provided choices to terminally ill Oregonians and has made Oregon a national leader in end-of-life care. The ODWDA is rarely used, but it has proven effective and safe for patients who choose physician-assisted suicide. These patients are well-educated, have health insurance, have hospice care available to them, and want to ensure a dignified death when they no longer can enjoy life. Congress may try yet again to overturn the Oregon law, but the current political climate may make it difficult to succeed in the attempt. Even if *Gonzales v. Oregon* has not removed the final obstacle for the Oregon Death With Dignity Act, the decision goes a long way in that direction.

> "*The primary reasons for requesting pre-scriptions for lethal medications were concern about loss of autonomy.*"

The Desire for Personal Autonomy Drives Assisted Suicide

Amy D. Sullivan, Katrina Hedberg, and David W. Fleming

Amy D. Sullivan, Katrina Hedberg, and David W. Fleming are physicians and public health experts. They produced this article in conjunction with their work for the Oregon Department of Health and Human Services, which is required to report on the practice of physician-assisted suicide in the state.

Sullivan, Hedberg, and Fleming gathered information on the impact of the Oregon Death with Dignity Act (ODWDA) from official reports as well as from interviews with physicians who prescribed drugs for suicide and family members of those who committed physician-assisted suicide. The report concentrates on the demographic characteristics of those terminally ill patients who use the physician-assisted suicide option. The numbers are small overall, although they were higher than the first year the ODWDA was in effect. More importantly, there was no indication that suicide was being forced on the poor or those without health insurance. On the contrary, those committing suicide with the aid of doctor-prescribed drugs were better educated than the overall population and thus probably better off economically. Financial considerations were not a major factor in the decision to

Amy D. Sullivan, Katrina Hedberg, and David W. Fleming, "Legalized Physician-Assisted Suicide in Oregon—The Second Year," *New England Journal of Medicine*, vol. 342, no. 8, February 24, 2000, pp. 598–604. Reproduced by permission.

commit suicide. Rather, these terminally ill patients stressed the desire to control their own manner of death.

We now report on the second year of experience with legalized physician-assisted suicide in Oregon, including information obtained from family members about the reasons for requests for assistance. . . .

Characteristics of Patients

The median age of the 27 patients who died [by ingesting lethal prescription medicine] in 1999 was 71 years.[1] They were similar to the 16 patients who died in 1998 with respect to demographic characteristics, underlying illnesses, use of hospice care, and health insurance coverage although a higher proportion of the patients who died in 1999 were married (44 percent vs. 12 percent in 1998). Sixty-three percent of the patients who died in 1999 had end-stage cancer—most commonly lung cancer—and 78 percent were enrolled in a hospice program before they died. . . .

In 1998, a total of 29,281 Oregon residents died, including 6994 who died of cancer and 76 who died of amyotrophic lateral sclerosis.[2] Using these 1998 data for comparison, we estimated that patients who ingested lethal medications in 1999 accounted for 9 of every 10,000 deaths and for 39 of every 10,000 deaths from cancer. In comparison, deaths from physician-assisted suicide in 1998 accounted for 6 of every 10,000 deaths and for 20 of every 10,000 deaths from cancer. The four patients with amyotrophic lateral sclerosis who died by assisted suicide in 1999 accounted for approximately 5 percent of deaths from this disease (none of the patients who died by assisted suicide in 1998 had amyotrophic lateral sclerosis). The patients who died by assisted suicide in 1999 resembled a cohort [group] of 6901 Oregon residents who

1. The median is the middle point. That is, half of the patients were under seventy-one years of age, half were over that age.
2. A degenerative neurological disease also known as Lou Gehrig's disease.

died from similar underlying illnesses, with respect to age, race, and residence. A higher level of education was associated with an increased likelihood of physician-assisted suicide. College graduates were more likely to die from physician-assisted suicide than were persons without a high-school education. . . .

No Evidence of Abuse of Poor

In 1999, 27 patients died after ingesting lethal medications prescribed under the Oregon Death with Dignity Act, as compared with 16 in 1998. A total of 33 patients received prescriptions for lethal doses of medication, as compared with 24 in 1998. Although concern about possible abuses persists, our data indicate that poverty, lack of education or health insurance, and poor care at the end of life were not important factors in patients' requests for assistance with suicide. Interviews with physicians and family members indicated that the primary reasons for requesting prescriptions for lethal medications were concern about loss of autonomy, concern about loss of control of bodily functions, an inability to participate in activities that make life enjoyable, physical suffering, and a determination to control the manner of death.

Patients who died by physician-assisted suicide were better educated but otherwise demographically similar to residents of Oregon with similar diseases who died in 1998. The low proportion of married persons in 1998 was not found in 1999. Although most of the patients spent their own funds on some medical expenses (e.g., for prescription drugs), all were insured for most other major medical expenses, often through a combination of Medicare and private supplemental policies.

Many patients who sought assistance with suicide had to ask more than one physician for a prescription for lethal medication. This finding is consistent with reports on the attitudes of physicians and medical students in Oregon toward physician-assisted suicide. Many physicians in the state are not willing to provide assistance with suicide. . . .

As best we could determine, all the physicians who provided assistance with suicide complied with the provisions of the Oregon Death With Dignity Act. Although the Oregon Health Division is not a regulatory agency for physicians, it does report any cases of noncompliance to the state Board of Medical Examiners. Underreporting cannot be assessed, and noncompliance is difficult to assess because of the possible repercussions for noncompliant physicians reporting data to the division.

Factors in the Decision to Commit Assisted Suicide

We found that patients' decisions to request assistance with suicide were based on several overlapping factors. Physical suffering was discussed by several family members as a cause of loss of autonomy, an inability to participate in activities that make life enjoyable, or a very poor quality of life. For example, one family member stated, "She would have stuck it out through the pain if she'd thought she'd get better [but believed that when] life has no meaning, it's no use hanging around." For a patient with amyotrophic lateral sclerosis, the feeling of being trapped by the disease contributed to concern about loss of autonomy. Family members frequently commented on loss of control of bodily functions when discussing loss of autonomy. The reasons for requesting a prescription sometimes overlapped to such an extent that they were difficult to categorize. Asked to cite the reasons for one patient's decision, a family member said, "It was everything; it was nothing." The responses of physicians and family members were similar and consistently pointed to patients' concern about the quality of life and their wish to have control over how they died.

When family members discussed a patient's concern about physical suffering, they referred to dyspnea [difficulty breathing] and dysphagia [inability to swallow], as well as pain.

Some patients were concerned that with adequate control of pain, the side effects of the pain medication would make life meaningless. Physical factors, especially dyspnea, have been identified as important predictors of a decrease in the will to live. However, among patients in Oregon, concern about physical suffering was not necessarily equivalent to the experience of suffering. Palliative care was available to all the patients who requested assistance with suicide, and three quarters of them received hospice care before they died.

Control over the Manner of Death

Many family members emphasized that the patient wanted to have control over how he or she died. One woman had purchased poison more than a decade before she died, when her cancer was first diagnosed, so that she would never be without the means of controlling the end of her life, should it become unbearable. Like many of the other patients, she was described as determined to have this kind of control. Another patient was described as a "gutsy woman" who was "determined in her lifetime and determined about [physician-assisted suicide]." Family members expressed profound grief over their loss. However, mixed with this grief was great respect for the patient's choice. One man said about his wife of almost 50 years, "She was my only girl; I didn't want to lose her . . . but she wanted to do this."

Organizations to Contact

The editors have compiled the following list of organizations concerned with the issues debated in this book. The descriptions are derived from materials provided by the organizations. All have publications or information available for interested readers. The list was compiled on the date of publication of the present volume; the information provided here may change. Be aware that many organizations take several weeks or longer to respond to inquiries, so allow as much time as possible.

American Medical Association (AMA)
515 N. State St., Chicago, IL   60610
(800) 621-8335
e-mail: amaa@ama-assn.org
Web site: www.ama-assn.org

Physicians face issues of life and death on a much more frequent basis than the general public. The AMA, the largest organization of physicians in the United States, issues guidelines on the ethics of end-of-life care and has even devised a model curriculum dealing with these issues. It has come out strongly against euthanasia.

Compassion and Choices
PO Box 101810, Denver, CO   80250-1810
(800) 247-7421 • fax: (303) 639-1224
e-mail: info@compassionandchoices.org
Web site: www.compassionandchoices.org

Compassion and Choices was formed from the merger of two longtime right-to-die organizations: Compassion in Dying and End-of-Life Choices. The group is a vigorous advocate for the passage of right-to-die legislation as well as the reform of medical standards in palliative and end-of-life care.

Death with Dignity National Center

520 SW Sixth Ave., Suite 1030, Portland, OR   97204
(503) 228-4415 • fax: (503) 228-7454
e-mail: info@deathwithdignity.org.
Web site: www.deathwithdignity.org

The Death with Dignity National Center began in an effort to pass the Oregon Death with Dignity Act in 1994. More recently the organization has been engaged in the court effort to protect the Oregon law as well as aiding efforts to pass similar laws in other states.

Euthanasia Research and Guidance Organization (ERGO)

24829 Norris Ln., Junction City, OR   97448-9559
(541) 998-1873 • fax: (541) 998-1873
e-mail: dhumphry@efn.org
Web site: www.finalexit.org

Largely the work of longtime euthanasia advocate Derek Humphry, ERGO is a clearinghouse for information on euthanasia laws around the world. In addition, it disseminates knowledge on new methods and technologies for assisted or unassisted "self-deliverance."

International Task Force on Euthanasia and Assisted Suicide

PO Box 760, Steubenville, OH   43952
(740) 282-3810
e-mail: rmarker@internationaltaskforce.org
Web site: www.internationaltaskforce.org

This organization functions as a clearinghouse for information on euthanasia laws around the world. It seeks to build an international network of anti-euthanasia campaigners. It also maintains a library of euthanasia-related materials. The organization's director makes frequent appearances in public debates on euthanasia.

National Hospice and Palliative Care Organization

1700 Diagonal Rd., Suite 625, Alexandria, VA   22314

(703) 837-1500 • fax: (703) 837-1233
e-mail: caringinfo@nhpco.org
Web site: www.caringinfo.org

Rather than focus on legislation, the National Hospice and Palliative Care Organization helps individuals and families prepare for end-of-life decisions. It offers information and advice on financial, medical, hospice care, and other issues faced by the terminally ill.

National Right to Life Committee
512 Tenth St. NW, Washington, DC   20004
(202) 626-8800
e-mail: nrlc@nrlc.org
Web site: www.nrlc.org

Known more for opposition to abortion, the National Right to Life Committee is also involved in related issues, including anti-euthanasia activities. It concentrates its efforts on "restoring the legal protection for innocent life in the United States."

Not Dead Yet
7521 Madison St., Forest Park, IL   60130
(708) 209-1500 • fax: (708) 209-1735
e-mail: ndycoleman@aol.com
Web site: www.notdeadyet.org

Not Dead Yet is an organization of disabled people who believe that legalization of euthanasia will lead to the devaluation of human life, especially of those with physical or mental handicaps. The organization is known for its lively protests against mercy killing.

Open Society Institute: Project on Death in America
400 W. Fifty-ninth St., New York, NY   10019
(212) 548-0600
e-mail: pdia@sorosny.org
Web site: www.soros.org/initiatives/pdia

Funded by billionaire George Soros, the Project on Death in America funds research into the social and medical aspects of the end-of-life debate in the United States. It also publicizes the results of the research it has funded.

For Further Research

Books

Susan M. Behuniak and Arthur G. Svenson, *Physician-Assisted Suicide. The Anatomy of a Constitutional Law Issue*. Lanham, MD: Rowman & Littlefield, 2003.

Donald W. Cox, *Hemlock's Cup: The Struggle for Death with Dignity*. Buffalo, NY: Prometheus, 1993.

David Cundiff, *Euthanasia Is Not the Answer: A Hospice Physician's View*. Totowa, NJ: Humana, 1992.

Lynne Curry, ed., *The Human Body on Trial: A Sourcebook with Cases, Laws, and Documents*. Santa Barbara, CA: ABC-CLIO, 2002.

Karen J. Donnelly, *Cruzan v. Missouri: The Right to Die*. New York: Rosen, 2004.

Ian Robert Dowbiggin, *A Concise History of Euthanasia: Life, Death, God, and Medicine*. Lanham, MD: Rowman & Littlefield, 2005.

Jon B. Eisenberg, *Using Terri: The Religious Right's Conspiracy to Take Away Our Rights*. San Francisco: HarperSanFrancisco, 2005.

Mark Fuhrman, *Silent Witness: The Untold Story of Terri Schiavo's Death*. New York: Morrow, 2005.

Daniel Hillyard and John Dembrink, *Dying Right: The Death with Dignity Movement*. New York: Routledge, 2001.

Leon R. Kass, *Life, Liberty, and the Defense of Dignity: The Challenge for Bioethics*. San Francisco: Encounter, 2002.

Jack Kevorkian, *Prescription: Medicide; The Goodness of Planned Death*. Buffalo, NY: Prometheus, 1991.

Robert Lee and Derek Morgan, eds., *Death Rites: Law and Ethics at the End of Life*. New York: Routledge, 1994.

Carol Loving, *My Son, My Sorrow: The Tragic Tale of Dr. Kevorkian's Youngest Patient*. Far Hills, NJ: New Horizon, 1998.

Daniel C. Maguire, *Death by Choice*. Garden City, NY: Doubleday, 1984.

Jonathan D. Moreno, ed., *Arguing Euthanasia: The Controversy over Mercy Killing, Assisted Suicide, and the "Right to Die."* New York: Simon & Schuster, 1995.

M. Scott Peck, *Denial of the Soul: Spiritual and Medical Perspectives on Euthanasia and Mortality*. New York: Harmony Books, 1997.

Constance E. Putnam, *Hospice or Hemlock? Searching for Heroic Compassion*. Westport, CT: Praeger, 2002.

Wesley J. Smith, *Forced Exit: The Slippery Slope from Assisted Suicide to Legalized Murder*. Dallas: Spence, 2003.

Michael M. Uhlmann, ed., *Last Rights? Assisted Suicide and Euthanasia Debated*. Washington, DC: Ethics and Public Policy Center, 1998.

Melvin I. Urofsky, *Lethal Judgments: Assisted Suicide and American Law*. Lawrence: University Press of Kansas, 2000.

Marjorie B. Zucker, ed., *The Right to Die Debate: A Documentary History*. Westport, CT: Greenwood, 1999.

Periodicals

Jeffrey Bell and Frank Cannon, "The Politics of the Schiavo Case," *Weekly Standard*, April 4, 2005.

Gloria Borger, "Life, Death, and Politics," *U.S. News & World Report*, November 2, 2003.

Barry A. Bostrom, *"Gonzales v. Oregon," Issues in Law & Medicine*, Spring 2006.

Alexander Morgan Capron, "Death and the Court," *Hastings Center Report*, September/October 1997.

Eric Chevlen, "Free to Die," *First Things: A Monthly Journal of Religion & Public Life*, August/September 1999.

Arthur E. Chin, Katrina Hedberg, Grant K. Higginson, and David W. Fleming, "Legalized Physician-Assisted Suicide in Oregon—the First Year's Experience," *New England Journal of Medicine*, February 18, 1999.

Christian Century, "Endings," April 19, 2005.

Adam J. Cohen, "The Open Door: Will the Right to Die Survive *Washington v. Glucksberg* and *Vacco v. Quill?*" *In the Public Interest*, no. 79, 1997.

Commonweal, "Allowing to Die," April 23, 2004.

John Corry, "Who Is Jack Kevorkian, Really?" *Reader's Digest*, April 1999.

Maureen M. Devlin, *"Quill v. Vacco," Issues in Law & Medicine*, Summer 1996.

Joan Didion, "The Case of Theresa Schiavo," *New York Review of Books*, June 9, 2005.

H. Tristram Engelhardt and Ana Smith Iltis, "End-of-Life: The Traditional Christian View," *Lancet*, September 17, 2005.

Ellen Wilson Fielding, "Jack the Reaper," *Human Life Review*, Winter 1997.

Steve Forbes, "Euthanasia by Stealth," *Forbes*, April 18, 2005.

Patricia Guthrie, "Assisted Suicide Debated in the United States," *Canadian Medical Association Journal*, March 14, 2006.

Nat Hentoff, "Whose Lives Are Worth Continuing?" *Human Life Review*, Winter 2004.

Human Events "Scalia Sharply Critical of Assisted Suicide," January 17, 1997.

Kenneth Jost, "'I Want to Stop It from Happening Again,'"*CQ Researcher*, May 13, 2005.

Rita L. Marker, "Euthanasia and Assisted Suicide Today," *Society*, May/June 2006.

Diane Martindale, "A Culture of Death," *Scientific American*, Jun2005, vol. 292 no. 6, p.44–46.

Mental Health Weekly "Expert: Oregon 'Death with Dignity' Act Opens Pandora's Box," November 21, 1994.

Martha Minow, "Which Question? Which Lie? Reflections on the Physician-Assisted Suicide Cases," *Supreme Court Review*. 1997.

Joseph P. Shapiro, "Dr. Death's Last Dance," *U.S. News & World Report*, April 26, 1999.

Wesley J. Smith, "Dr. Death's Mouthpiece Mouths Off," *Human Life Review*, Fall 1998.

Elise Soukup, "Beyond Euthanasia," *Newsweek*, July 12, 2004.

Laura Spinney, "Last Rights," *New Scientist*, April 23, 2005.

Supreme Court Debates "The Right to Die," December 2005.

David Van Biema and Elaine Lafferty, "Is There a Right to Die?" *Time*, January 13, 1997.

Stephen Vincent, "A Protocol for Medical Murder," *Human Life Review*, Fall 2005.

Wilson Quarterly "Dr. Death Is a Quack," Summer 1997.

Adam Wolfson, "Killing Off the Dying?" *Public Interest*, Spring 1998.

Richard L. Worsnop, "Assisted Suicide Controversy," *CQ Researcher*, May 5, 1995.

Web Sites

BBC News Background Briefings: Euthanasia (http:// news.bbc.co.uk/1/hi/health/background_briefings/ euthanasia/default.stm). This Web site, from the prestigious British Broadcasting Corporation, is a good source for putting the euthanasia debate into a global perspective. While the site focuses on British cases, it contains a variety of articles detailing other nations' experiences with euthanasia laws. The site also contains a useful glossary of terms used in the controversy over euthanasia.

Euthanasia and Physician Assisted Suicide: All Sides (www.religioustolerance.org/euthanas.htm). This Canadian-based Web site offers views of euthanasia from a religious, yet nondenominational, perspective. It has a handy set of links to the current status of euthanasia laws in Canada, the United States, Great Britain, and elsewhere in the world.

Euthanasia and the Right to Die (www.trinity.edu/~mkearl/ dtheuth.html). Although old, this site contains a wealth of active links to both proponents and opponents of assisted suicide and euthanasia. Produced by sociologist Michael Kearl at Trinity University in Texas, the site also includes data and analysis from social surveys on public attitudes toward euthanasia.

Frontline: The Kevorkian Verdict (www.pbs.org/wgbh/ pages/frontline/kevorkian). This site, produced by the Boston Public Broadcasting affiliate WGBH, has detailed information on the life of Jack Kevorkian. It also includes legal analysis of the court cases involving Kevorkian as well as links to audio interviews with Kevorkian's patients and their families.

Onpolitics.com Supreme Court—Key Cases 1996–1997
(www.washingtonpost.com/wp-srv/national/longterm/
supcourt/1996-97/assist96.htm). Arguably, the years 1996
and 1997 were the height of the debate over euthanasia in
the United States. The Oregon Death with Dignity Act
went into effect and the two key Supreme Court cases,
Quill v. Vacco and *Washington v. Glucksberg* were decided. This site contains links to *Washington Post* articles
on the Oregon law as well as the full text of the Supreme
Court decisions. Linked articles also describe the public
controversy over the issue at the time.

Index